"You were my girl, Carole Anne. Mine. In here."

Jeff tapped a finger on the center of her chest, touching the center of her soul. When she turned away, he caught her by the shoulders. "You were mine. As much mine as I was yours."

Carole Anne wanted to pull away, but she couldn't. He held her fast, imprisoning her very soul with the look in his eyes.

She tried to make him understand now what she couldn't make him understand then. "Don't you see? I didn't want to stay here. You did. I wanted to try my wings and soar."

He released her. "So, you've soared. Is it as wonderful as you thought?"

No, there were disappointments, at times so overwhelming she didn't think she could bear it. And there were nights, nights when she felt devastatingly alone and lost.

But she couldn't admit that to Jeff. "Yes," she said stubbornly. "It's wonderful."

Dear Reader,

At Silhouette Romance we're celebrating the start of 1994 with a wonderful lineup of exciting love stories. Get set for a year filled with terrific books by the authors you love best, and brand-new names you'll be delighted to discover.

Those FABULOUS FATHERS continue, with Linc Rider in Kristin Morgan's *Rebel Dad*. Linc was a mysterious drifter who entered the lives of widowed Jillian Fontenot and her adopted son. Little did Jillian know he was a father in search of a child—*her* child.

Pepper Adams is back with *Lady Willpower*. In this charming battle of wills, Mayor Joe Morgan meets his match when Rachel Fox comes to his town and changes it—and Joe!

It's a story of love lost and found in Marie Ferrarella's *Aunt Connie's Wedding*. Carole Anne Wellsley was home for her aunt's wedding, and Dr. Jefferson Drumm wasn't letting her get away again!

And don't miss Rebecca Daniels's *Loving the Enemy*. This popular Intimate Moments author brings her special brand of passion to the Silhouette Romance line. Rounding out the month, look for books by Geeta Kingsley and Jude Randal.

We hope that you'll be joining us in the coming months for books by Diana Palmer, Elizabeth August, Suzanne Carey and many more of your favorite authors.

Anne Canadeo
Senior Editor

Please address questions and book requests to:
Reader Service
U.S.: P.O. Box 1325, Buffalo, NY 14269
Canadian: P.O. Box 1050, Niagara Falls, Ont. L2E 7G7

AUNT CONNIE'S WEDDING
Marie Ferrarella

Silhouette
ROMANCE™
Published by Silhouette Books
America's Publisher of Contemporary Romance

If you purchased this book without a cover you should be aware that this book is stolen property. It was reported as "unsold and destroyed" to the publisher, and neither the author nor the publisher has received any payment for this "stripped book."

To Carole Anne Yinquez.
Here's your happy ending,
as promised.

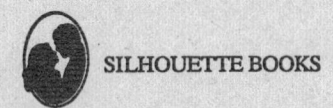

SILHOUETTE BOOKS

ISBN 0-373-08984-8

AUNT CONNIE'S WEDDING

Copyright © 1994 by Marie Rydzynski-Ferrarella

All rights reserved. Except for use in any review, the reproduction or utilization of this work in whole or in part in any form by any electronic, mechanical or other means, now known or hereafter invented, including xerography, photocopying and recording, or in any information storage or retrieval system, is forbidden without the written permission of the editorial office, Silhouette Books, 300 East 42nd Street, New York, NY 10017 U.S.A.

All characters in this book have no existence outside the imagination of the author and have no relation whatsoever to anyone bearing the same name or names. They are not even distantly inspired by any individual known or unknown to the author, and all incidents are pure invention.

This edition published by arrangement with Harlequin Enterprises B.V.

® and TM are trademarks of Harlequin Enterprises B.V., used under license. Trademarks indicated with ® are registered in the United States Patent and Trademark Office, the Canadian Trade Marks Office and in other countries.

Printed in U.S.A.

Books by Marie Ferrarella

Silhouette Romance

The Gift #588
Five-Alarm Affair #613
Heart to Heart #632
Mother for Hire #686
Borrowed Baby #730
Her Special Angel #744
The Undoing of Justin Starbuck #766
Man Trouble #815
The Taming of the Teen #839
Father Goose #869
Babies on His Mind #920
The Right Man #932
In Her Own Backyard #947
Her Man Friday #959
Aunt Connie's Wedding #984

Silhouette Special Edition

It Happened One Night #597
A Girl's Best Friend #652
Blessing in Disguise #675
Someone To Talk To #703
World's Greatest Dad #767
Family Matters #832
She Got Her Man #843

Silhouette Intimate Moments

*Holding Out for a Hero #496
*Heroes Great and Small #501
*Christmas Every Day #538

*Those Sinclairs!

Silhouette Books

Silhouette Christmas Stories 1992
"The Night Santa Claus Returned"

Books by Marie Ferrarella writing as Marie Nicole

Silhouette Romance

Man Undercover #373
Please Stand By #394
Mine by Write #411
Getting Physical #440

Silhouette Desire

Tried and True #112
Buyer Beware #142
Through Laughter and Tears #161
Grand Theft: Heart #182
A Woman of Integrity #197
Country Blue #224
Last Year's Hunk #274
Foxy Lady #315
Chocolate Dreams #346
No Laughing Matter #382

MARIE FERRARELLA

was born in Europe, raised in New York City and now lives in Southern California. She describes herself as the tired mother of two overenergetic children and the contented wife of one wonderful man. She is thrilled to be following her dream of writing full-time.

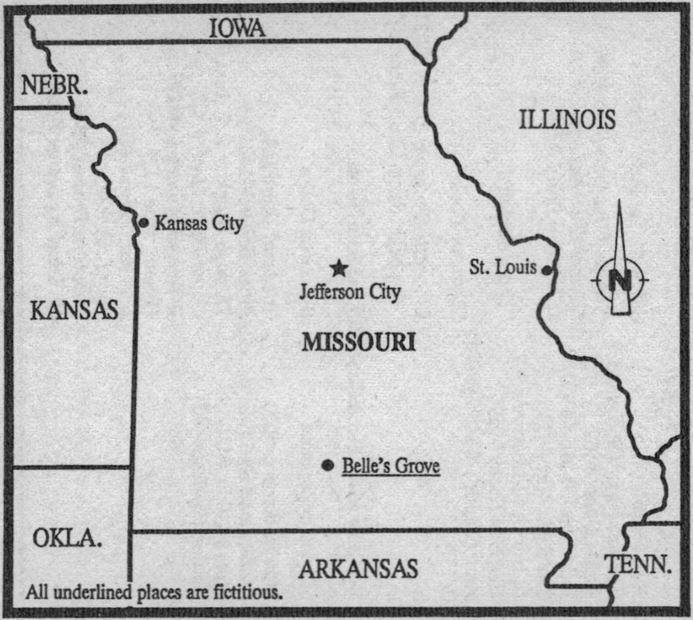
IOWA
NEBR.
ILLINOIS
Kansas City
KANSAS
St. Louis
N
Jefferson City
MISSOURI
Belle's Grove
OKLA.
ARKANSAS
TENN.
All underlined places are fictitious.

Chapter One

The entire drive from the airport had been like taking one giant step backward in time. Everything was still the same. Eight years and the town hadn't changed.

Only she had.

Carole Anne Wellsley guided the rented silver car toward her aunt's house. She felt as if she were moving in slow motion, as if every inch was somehow elongating itself like a cat stretching before the winter fire.

And then there was no more road left. No more excuses. Joy and anxiety bobbed and weaved within her, tossing the rest of her emotions back and forth like a volleyball over a net during a heated tournament. She was glad to finally be here; she wanted to be two thousand miles away, safely at her desk, working on another article.

It's going to be all right. You're making yourself crazy for no reason.

Carole Anne took a deep, steadying breath. The July air felt hot and sticky. No, nothing had changed.

Pulling on the door handle, she forced herself to leave the shelter of the car. The Missouri sun shone down on her, warm and patient. Carole Anne moved around the front of the car and opened the passenger door.

"Come on out, honey. We're here." She laced oddly cold fingers around Brandon's as he tumbled from his seat.

Drawing support from the contact, she turned and faced the front of the house squarely, a soldier confronting the unknown. Or worse, the known. Carole Anne stood where she was.

"Mom," Brandon's voice squeaked, "you're squeezing all the blood out."

Carole Anne's lips rose in an apologetic smile as she loosened her hold on her son's hand. She cleared her throat self-consciously. She'd been trying to instill Brandon with a steely streak of independence. Seeing uneasiness in his mother's eyes would undoubtedly set her efforts back by a few months.

She tossed her head slightly and her curly pale blond hair swayed from side to side. "Sorry." The smile was now careless and full of bravado.

Brandon was staring straight ahead and had apparently missed his mother's performance for his sake. He squinted against the bright sun. "This it?"

She couldn't tell if he was disappointed or not. "This is it."

Brandon Wellsley took a long, penetrating look around, carefully appraising his surroundings. He was far more quiet than the average six-year-old, far more introspective. Being the only male in his mother's life had made him assume the mantle of solemnity light-years too soon. Carole Anne worried about that.

Brandon looked back over his shoulder. The road leading to the huge three-story house was tree-lined. Tall oaks had bent sage green heads toward one another on either side, like sentries whispering a secret as they had traveled on it. Their conference had allowed only fragments of the sun to filter through. Brandon felt as if he were on an adventure. The house was like nothing he had ever seen before. Back home in Southern California, they lived near the beach. In his neighborhood, the cubelike houses were bright and cheerful. They made him think of a row of Lego blocks waiting to be played with.

The house that now stood before them looked as if it had always been here, maybe even before the dinosaurs. It looked old, but not sad, the way Tommy Anderson's grandfather did. This looked like a nice old, Brandon decided. A pretty old. It was a forever house. It made Brandon feel all grown up just to be near it.

He cocked his shaggy, light brown head, then scratched it. Then he turned from the house and looked carefully at his mother.

"You really lived here?"

She nodded. "For sixteen years."

As she said it, Carole Anne could almost *feel* each one of those sixteen years vibrating through her, connecting with some link she had long since thought buried. She had traveled two thousand miles since this morning just to get here.

So why are you having such trouble crossing the last twenty feet, Carole Anne? she demanded impatiently of herself. What ghosts was she afraid to see? There were no ghosts. Only the living.

Especially one.

A spark entered Brandon's eyes as he saw an old swing hanging from a branch on an oak tree, eternally tethered there, sashaying gently to and fro in the breeze. He had a shiny swing set in his manicured backyard at home, but the swing, perhaps because of its age, seemed to have a special allure.

Debating testing it out, Brandon took a step toward it, only to discover that he was still being held fast by his mother. He sighed and stayed put.

"How come you left?" he wanted to know.

For a hundred different reasons. Because I wanted to fly instead of walk. Because I couldn't breathe here. Because I had to see what was over the next hill, the next rainbow.

"Because I loved your dad and he was on his way to California." She smiled for his benefit and looked down into eyes that so clearly echoed her own. "Remember? I've told you that story a hundred times." Ninety-nine times at the boy's request, usually at bedtime, she thought with a smile.

The small head bobbed up and down, his mind already racing onward. "Yeah, I 'member." He tugged on his mother's hand impatiently. "So, c'mon," Brandon urged when the tug didn't generate the desired result. "Are we going to meet Aunt Connie or not?"

His eyes strayed once more to the swing. The sooner he got to meet everyone he was supposed to meet, the sooner he could change clothes and play. The jacket his mother had forced him to wear on the flight over was hot and felt confining, like a heavy, coarse wool blanket. He was dying to get out of it, but hadn't said anything because he had sensed his mother's nervousness. Her unspoken agitation fueled his own unease. His mother was *never* nervous about anything, except spiders. Just what was this Aunt Connie like?

Inertia mounted, pouring lead through her limbs, pressing her feet to the ground as she looked toward the house. It wasn't fear of Aunt Connie that was holding her back. It was fear of all the rest of it. Memories with a capital M.

Carole Anne shook her head, trying to dispel the confusion that had been her constant companion since she had received Aunt Connie's chatty letter with its almost throwaway postscript. She was getting married and would Carole Anne be a dear and come help her with the wedding preparations?

Just like that, with no preamble, no discourse after. Nothing. But that was the way Aunt Connie was. Her mind was always in a hundred different places at once. By the time

Carole Anne had caught up to her on one subject, Aunt Connie had already gone on to the next, never covering anything fully enough for Carole Anne's satisfaction.

Carole Anne had almost choked when she read the words. An immediate follow-up phone call to Aunt Connie had shed no more light on the subject, except that the older woman was ecstatically happy and excited. Despite her efforts, Carole Anne had gotten no more information out of the sweet old dear about the groom-to-be than his name and the fact that he had broad shoulders. Aunt Connie had gotten caught up in talking about cookies and flower arrangements at the reception.

Frustrated, concerned, Carole Anne booked a flight out for the following weekend.

She felt Brandon tug on her hand again. He was still waiting for an answer. Her mind was wandering again. Carole Anne shook off her mood.

"We're going to meet Aunt Connie," she told him. "Or at least, you are." Big blue eyes narrowed slightly and looked at her questioningly. Carole Anne smiled. "I've already met her, remember?"

She had been younger than Brandon when she had first met Aunt Connie. The woman was really her great aunt... and her mother and father from the time she was four years old. Aunt Connie had taken Carole Anne into her spacious house and her spacious heart within hours of her parents' fatal accident—two very young people and an insane race with a train at a railroad crossing that hadn't been won.

Before Carole Anne had a chance to say anything else, the door to the stately Victorian house opened. A short, stout woman with short, platinum-tinted hair, dressed in an impossibly flirty yellow dress, emerged. Even from twenty feet away, her smile radiated warmth that competed with the sun overhead and drew the two people in her yard toward her.

Connie Jenkins threw out her arms in a familiar gesture that was forever imprinted on Carole Anne's heart. Suddenly she was ten again, rushing home from school, drawn by the smell of freshly baked chocolate-chip cookies and the soft scent of vanilla that was as much Aunt Connie as her cherubic smile and sparkling blue eyes.

Carole Anne warned herself not to allow the feeling to seep into her too extensively. This was just a visit to a place that had been home once, but not now. Home was somewhere else now. And that was just the way she wanted it.

Connie shook her head, her high-pitched laugh echoing in the air, her platinum hair shimmying to and fro against her round face.

"Certainly took you two long enough to get here!" she called to them. She took the two steps down the porch to reach the ground. "Give me a hug, both of you!" she commanded.

Within a moment, there was no distance left between them at all. Taking his cue from his mother, Brandon raced her to reach Aunt Connie.

Connie Jenkins, with the agility of a woman half her age, dropped to her knees to hug the little boy she had never seen except in the photographs that Carole Anne sent faithfully with each long letter. Photographs that lined the walls of her parlor.

Tears brimming in her eyes, Connie couldn't ask for more happiness than she had at this very moment. "My, but you are a handsome boy," she pronounced, her soft voice quavering slightly as she held him tightly against her ample bosom.

"And you're a very strong lady," Brandon said with equal aplomb.

"Holding you too tight, am I?" Connie laughed. She loosened her arms slightly, but kept him against her for a moment longer. This had been a long time in coming and she intended to savor it.

"Yes, ma'am," Brandon agreed guilelessly. "Like Mom." He turned his head toward his mother. "She almost squeezed my fingers off when we got out of the car."

Connie rose to her feet slowly, brushing off her knees. She turned toward Carole Anne. The bright blue eyes misted behind her rimless glasses, but she didn't bother wiping them away. They were good tears, cleansing tears, and there was nothing to be ashamed of.

She didn't bother wondering what there was to fear and why her niece would squeeze her son's hand because she was about to enter the house she had abandoned so long ago, the house where she had grown up. It was only important that she was here now. The years before melted away and were lost, like dew disappearing beneath the warming rays of the rising sun.

Connie threw her arms around Carole Anne and held her close. "Welcome home, Carole Anne." Her voice was thick with feeling.

Guilt nettled her for having waited so long. Carole Anne resisted succumbing to it and to the feeling seeping into her body, the desire to let herself be carried away and be cared for by this wonderful woman. She was an adult now, not a child.

But she didn't resist returning the hug. That would have involved superhuman effort. "I'm only here for a visit," she reminded the woman. "Just long enough to check out the man who won your heart and to help you with the wedding arrangements...if he passes my inspection."

Aunt Connie stood back and took her niece's hands into her own. Carole Anne remembered how soft her hands had always felt, how gentle. Nostalgia wound all through her, despite the windows and doors she had futilely barred against all this.

Connie smiled patiently. Carole Anne seemed skittish, but she'd settle down soon enough. Things always had a way of working themselves out.

"I'd still welcome you home, even if it was for just five minutes." Her eyes indicated the house behind her. "This'll always be home, no matter where you go. No matter for how long."

Carole Anne knew it was useless to argue with Aunt Connie's pronouncement. It seemed pointless to remind her aunt that her home was now elsewhere. She hadn't come this far to argue with the woman she had loved her entire life. Besides, it wasn't Aunt Connie she would have been arguing with. Carole Anne knew she would have been arguing with that small, nagging "something" within her, something as tiny as a chick-pea hiding in the darkest corner of the barn. Something that agreed with what Aunt Connie said. That this was home.

But it wasn't. Not anymore. Perhaps not ever. She had never managed to feel a hundred percent comfortable here. A part of her had always felt as if she was just marking time. Waiting. A prizefighter straining to hear the bell go off for a round, a bell that signaled the beginning of excitement, not endless tranquillity.

She had left like that, waiting to have her life take off. She had left town because destiny and Cal Wellsley had beckoned to her, promising something that Belle's Grove could never deliver.

Carole Anne saw her aunt's eyes regarding her thoughtfully. Aunt Connie was up in the air most of the time, but she had an uncanny way of cutting to the heart of the matter like an expert surgeon making an incision in exactly the right place every time. She didn't want to hear questions right now.

Carole Anne squeezed Aunt Connie's hands affectionately. "So, who is this dashing swashbuckler who's swept you off your feet, and when do I meet him?"

Connie gave her a pleased smile that generously spilled down to Brandon as her gaze took him in, as well. "How does now sound?"

"Now?" Carole Anne's smile sagged at the corners of her mouth. She glanced down at her navy business suit. She wanted to change, to look better just in case— She squelched the thought. It was normal to want to look presentable to *anyone.* "Aunt Connie, I've just traveled two thousand miles—"

If there was a protest in her niece's voice, Connie took no notice of it. "And never looked better." She looked to the boy for corroboration. "Doesn't she look good, Brandon?"

Brandon shrugged, small, thin shoulders rising and falling beneath the blue gabardine material. It was a gesture that was reminiscent of his mother. "I suppose so."

"See, unbiased testimony. There's absolutely nothing to fret about." Connie hooked one arm through Carole Anne's and effectively locked her in place. "Emmett's just inside the front parlor."

Carole Anne felt dusty and tired and would have killed for a cold soda. The summer heat was already weaving a closed, oppressive net around her, making her long for air conditioning. But she might as well get to the heart of the matter now instead of later. After all, Emmett Carson and his designs on her aunt's heart was why she had traveled all this way so quickly. If not for him, who knew when she would have returned, if ever.

"All right." She had learned long ago that flighty or not, Aunt Connie always found a way to get what she wanted. She'd hammer relentlessly at the obstacle until it fell away. Carole Anne smiled warmly at her aunt. "Let's meet your prince charming."

"That's my girl." Connie patted Carole Anne's hand approvingly, still keeping what was, for all intents and purposes, a death grip on her arm. Then turning slightly, she took hold of Brandon's hand and marched them both to the front door.

It was wonderful to feel a small hand placed within hers again. Both hands occupied, Connie blinked away another tear.

"Open the door for us, Brandon," she prompted. "Gentlemen always hold doors open for ladies."

"Mom says everyone should open their own doors," Brandon responded automatically, parroting an axiom his mother had repeatedly told him. But he did as he was asked.

Connie turned the notion over in her mind for a moment. "At times," she agreed as Brandon yanked the door open.

Carole Anne opened her mouth to say that it should be at all times, that no one should expect to be helped by anyone else for any reason. It was something she had painfully learned since she had left the sheltering oaks of Belle's Grove. Something Cal had taught her without meaning to.

But all the eloquent words at her disposal broke apart into minuscule particles.

Her eyes widened as she stared. The front room of Connie Jenkins's two-hundred-year-old home was filled with people. Townspeople. Old ones, young ones. People she had grown up with. There must have been thirty, perhaps forty people there.

She didn't see any of them clearly. Individual bodies were like designs on a paisley print, melded to form a vague whole, a background. She saw only one figure. Only one face.

And all the ghosts she had been afraid of converged into one entity.

Jefferson Drumm.

He knew that if he held on to his tall glass of frosted pink lemonade any tighter, it would shatter, leaving him with a handful of ice cubes and trickling pink liquid, not to mention cuts and pain.

Not unlike the way he had felt the morning after he had found out that she had gone, Jefferson thought. Only intense concentration kept every muscle within his face in repose as his eyes swept over her now.

She was beautiful.

The long-haired girl who had left Belle's Grove and him eight years ago had been pretty, a wildflower to be discovered in the meadow. The woman who stood in the doorway now was a rose in full bloom. The first blush was gone, but it was all the more beautiful for that.

All the old feelings rose up within Jefferson, advancing to engage in a war with the steely bands of tranquillity he had forged around his life after she had gone and taken the sun with her.

He had wanted to come today; only death would have kept him away.

It very nearly had, what with Simon Barlow stumbling into the clinic this morning with his arm completely swollen and stiff. The stoic fool had come within a hairsbreadth of having his arm amputated. All because of his desire to shrug off the "inconvenience" of injuries and pain.

Men like Simon made Jefferson's medical practice a challenge, even in this enlightened day and age. They belonged in the Dark Ages. He had given Simon two injections, cleaned the wound and stitched him up. He had repeated the dosage for Simon's medication to Simon's young daughter three times and hoped it sank in. Then he'd changed quickly and hurried to Connie's house, the last to arrive.

Jefferson wasn't thinking of Simon now, though. As he'd stood, waiting for her to arrive, he had been thinking of Carole Anne. Of the way she had felt in his arms as they danced in the moonlight at her high school prom. Of the way her lips had felt, eager and shy at the same time, when he had kissed her for the first time. Of the way he had felt, wanting her, making plans night after night as he lay awake in his dorm, only to return to Belle's Grove and discover that she had run off with Cal Wellsley, his friend. His best friend. The guy he had asked to look after Carole Anne while he was away at school.

A multitude of emotions had raced through him that day. Rage, anger, a sense of betrayal. And pain. Dark, overwhelming pain.

But it hadn't consumed him and he had gone on to vanquish it, to get his degree, hang up his shingle here in the town she had professed to loathe. And gone on with his life.

Or so he had thought. Life took an entirely brighter turn as she walked through the door.

Jefferson smiled at her as she looked in his direction. His lips felt like small, tight rubber bands stretched to the limit. What was she thinking? he wondered. Did she feel anything at all?

He moved forward, until he stood directly in front of her. She still wore the same cologne. He tried not to let that distract him. And failed.

"Carole Anne."

His voice rumbled through her system, barging in, creating a spasm in her stomach. She almost splayed her hand over it, but stopped herself in time.

No, she wasn't twenty anymore, she reminded herself. She was a twenty-eight-year-old woman, unaffected by such things as the sound of a man's voice. Even a man she had once cared for, or thought she had, she amended shakily. That was for children, not her.

But it didn't help that Jefferson had grown from appealingly pleasant-looking to vitally handsome in the span of eight years. It didn't help that his face had become more chiseled with the imprint of character, his eyes greener, his mouth firmer and somehow more sensual. He wore his dark brown hair longer now. It curled invitingly against the back of his bronzed neck.

She found herself staring. He was so much more vivid than she remembered.

Carole Anne realized that people were looking at them and she forced a friendly, noncommittal smile to her lips as she extended her hand coolly to him. "What do I call you now? Dr. Drumm?"

"'Jeff' always worked for me."

Jefferson took her hand in his. She was nervous, he thought. As his fingers had brushed against her wrist, he'd felt her pulse jumping. She was afraid of him, he realized. Why, in God's name? He had never been anything but kind and considerate around her.

Maybe, he mused ruefully, still holding her hand, if he had been brash, brooding and dramatic, the way Cal had, she wouldn't have run off.

Exercising stress management techniques she had learned to cope with the tensions of being a single mother raising a child in a fast-paced world, Carole Anne forced herself to relax a fraction of an inch. Her thoughts halted as her eyes looked up into his. All the techniques blew up in front of her. They carried no weight here. She was back on nature's terms.

His smile, as it opened up, taking his eyes with it, did more than any six-week course in stress management had ever accomplished. Even when she was nervous, there had always been something about Jefferson that set her at ease. Being with him when he smiled that way was like feeling herself sliding into a warm bubble bath.

She was peripherally aware that the other people in the room had circled around them. Brandon had taken her hand again, drawing closer to her.

"So, how have you been, Jeff?" she asked a little too breezily.

"Busy." Jefferson looked down at the boy next to her. He extended his hand to him, one man to another. "Hello, Brandon."

Carole Anne's eyes narrowed as her son solemnly shook Jefferson's hand. "How did you know his name?"

The boy had eyes like his mother's, Jefferson noted. The rest belonged to Cal. He glanced at Carole Anne. "I kept tabs."

"I told him, darling," Aunt Connie interrupted, her cheery voice lightening the sudden tension she neither knew nor would have understood. She placed herself between the two, an unwitting referee. "Everyone in town knows Brandon's name. At least—" she waved a hand around the room and laughed "—the people who know me. And everyone reads your articles and has your books. The April issue of *The Journal* sold out the minute it hit the stands," she told her niece with pride. She literally beamed. "We're all so proud of you."

With one arm around her, she hugged Carole Anne to her. "Now, you just have to meet Emmett." With that, she led her away.

"That's why I'm here." Carole Anne looked over her shoulder and saw Jeff watching her, a thoughtful look in his eyes. A shiver of anticipation wriggled down her spine before she had a chance to shake it.

She was being silly. There was nothing to anticipate. Whatever had been was gone. She had been the one to signal the death knell herself. Whatever else might be true of her, she had always been one to take full responsibility for her actions. When she'd left Belle's Grove—and Jefferson Drumm—behind, she had known then that it was to be forever. And nothing was going to change that now.

She turned away and, smile in place, returned greetings from the others who had gathered within Aunt Connie's house to see her again. She couldn't manage, though, to shut out the feeling that Jeff's eyes were skimming over her, studying her.

Nor could she rid herself of the feeling that something was going to happen in this little overgrown, backwater town where nothing noteworthy ever really happened.

Something.

And it wasn't going to be just Aunt Connie's wedding.

Chapter Two

"And this, darling, is the most romantic man on the face of the earth."

With a flourish that would have seemed comical had anyone else executed it, Aunt Connie gestured toward the tall, stately, white-haired man standing a few feet away from them.

Carole Anne noted that he was watching them as they approached, amusement accenting the small, thin lips, what there was of them to see. A snow-white mustache drooped over his lips as it extended its wings to merge with equally wide sideburns. The deep-set brown eyes that peered out of all this whiteness lent themselves more handily to a man possessed of an elfin soul rather than that of a Valentino. They seemed to actually twinkle as her aunt drew closer.

Emmett Carson inclined his leonine head in a Continental movement as he nodded a greeting toward Carole Anne. But even though he was looking at her, Carole Anne had the distinct impression that all his attention was for the woman beside her. "Constance flatters me."

"Constance," Aunt Connie sighed, blissfully transported back over more than half a century. "I haven't been called that since I was a young girl."

Emmett enveloped Aunt Connie's hand in both of his, long graceful hands forming a haven to which she seemed to naturally gravitate. "An occurrence merely a few years in the past."

Aunt Connie inclined her head toward her niece. There was absolutely no mistaking the youthful joy radiating from her. "See why I love him?"

Her smile was polite, distant, as Carole Anne regarded the man beside her aunt with a suspicious reserve that had become second nature to her since she had left Belle's Grove. It wasn't good, she had learned, to take things at face value alone. Especially things that appeared to be too good to be true.

Carole Anne offered her hand to Emmett guardedly. "Hello, I'm—"

"Carole Anne," Emmett concluded. He smiled, amused at the young woman's self-introduction, considering the fact that this was her welcome home party. The mustache rose slightly on his gaunt cheeks. "Yes, I know."

Rather than shake her hand, he bowed and pressed a kiss to it ever so lightly. The mustache tickled, momentarily distracting her. "It's a pleasure to finally meet you."

We'll see, Carole Anne thought. "Thank you," she murmured as she dropped her hand to her side. She looked on as Emmett solemnly made Brandon's acquaintance. Brandon puffed up his chest at being treated like an adult.

He did *seem* nice, she thought. But Carole Anne intended to do a little investigating before passing judgment. Her aunt wasn't a wealthy woman, but she did own the house and had more than a comfortable amount set aside in the bank. Carole Anne didn't want to see the woman bilked out of her life savings by some good-looking man with a golden tongue and a few impressive mannerisms. Sharper women had been parted from their money by slick con men and, as far as Carole Anne was concerned, Aunt Connie had always been far too trusting and just a little vague when it came to reality.

Aunt Connie shifted slightly so that she was beside Emmett, who slipped his arm around the woman's shoulders so easily it could have been mistaken for a habit of long standing.

"Do you know how he proposed?" Aunt Connie's eyes sparkled as she looked up at Emmett.

She sounded like a schoolgirl, Carole Anne thought. Aunt Connie sounded, she thought with a touch of wistful envy, a great deal younger at this moment than she felt herself.

By now there was a sizable crowd all around them. Everyone was sharing vicariously in the conversation as well as the sentiment being expressed. Everyone, Carole Anne knew, loved Aunt Connie.

Emmett cleared his throat. Carole Anne thought she saw a flicker of what appeared to be genuine embarrassment in his eyes. He waved a thin hand in the air, as if pushing aside Aunt Connie's question. "Constance, I don't think this is the time—"

Aunt Connie just snuggled a little closer to him, her arm tucked around his waist. "Everyone else has already heard it, Emmett."

Yes, Carole Anne thought, knowing Aunt Connie, everyone within a ten-mile radius of Belle's Grove probably had. No sense in depriving the older woman of her moment of joy.

"How?" Carole Anne asked.

There were some faces that became animated with a smile. Connie Jenkins had that kind of a face. She seemed to glow now as she relived the tiniest of details in her mind.

"He got down on one knee and asked me for two favors." She paused for effect. It lasted less than half a beat, which was about as long as she could manage to maintain silence. "To first do him the favor of becoming his wife. And when I said yes, which of course I did immediately, he asked me to do him the favor of helping him up." She laughed and clapped her hands together before her lips, pleased as a child winning a coveted blue ribbon at the fair. She winked at Carole Anne. "If he hadn't won my heart before that, he did then."

Her aunt was completely, utterly, head over heels in love. It was there in the woman's eyes for all the world to see. If Emmett Carson was intent on taking advantage of her aunt for his own selfish gain, she'd personally skin him alive.

"I'm not as agile as I used to be," Emmett confessed to Carole Anne, addressing her as if the others weren't in the room. "Not like Constance is."

The broad wink that passed between the future bride and groom jolted Carole Anne and had her speculating on a subject that had heretofore never even absently crossed her mind.

Aunt Connie?

No, it wasn't possible. She'd never pictured the woman as having any sort of yearnings other than for mint-chip ice cream, her number one weakness and vice. Carole Anne drew a breath and took a step back, as if that could make her see things more clearly.

Connie seemed not to notice that her niece was one shade paler than she had been when she'd first greeted her. With an affectionate pat on the younger woman's elbow, Aunt Connie turned her attention to the crowd.

"And now that you've met my Mr. Right, why don't you mingle?" Connie gestured about the room, taking care not to hit anyone. People littered the area like so many leaves in autumn. "These are all your friends. You have so much catching up to do, dear."

As if a signal had gone off, the people around them seemed to press forward as Connie and Emmett eased out of the nucleus of the circle. Voices began to merge and overlap.

Carole Anne felt a headache spreading out probing tentacles on either side of her temples as suddenly the floodgates opened and questions began coming at her from all sides. People she had gone to school with, attended pajama parties with, played ball with, even distant acquaintances she couldn't readily place, all seemed to want an update on her life and her career, beginning from the moment she'd left the sleepy burg.

Trying to filter out the extraneous voices and make sense out of the questions, Carole Anne's hand tightened around Brandon's. She felt the boy pressing closer to her side.

She saw Aunt Connie waving at her to catch her attention. The woman temporarily reclaimed the space she had vacated at her niece's side. She took Brandon's free hand in hers.

"I have some chocolate cake I'd like to introduce him to," her aunt informed her, smiling down at Brandon. "And there are some children just about Brandon's age for him to meet."

Brandon hesitated a moment, turning uncertain blue eyes in his mother's direction.

Carole Anne felt that Brandon was far too attached to her. She was always looking for ways to painlessly urge him to dive into life's mainstream. But now a protective instinct had her wanting to gather the boy to her and hold him close.

Aunt Connie read the signs and knew what was necessary. She had uncanny radar when it came to children's actual needs. She wasn't about to be deterred.

"He'll be fine, Carole Anne," Aunt Connie assured her, separating mother and child. "You do like chocolate, don't you, dear?"

Brandon nodded.

"See?" she said over her shoulder to Carole Anne. "We'll get along fine, you and I," she told Brandon, ushering him away. "What do you think of mint-chip ice cream?"

Carole Anne couldn't hear Brandon's answer as someone behind her asked her just how far Los Angeles was from attaining permanent grid lock.

Even though she was in the center of a group of people, Carole Anne was aware of Jefferson's casual glance every time it drifted toward her. The crowd had eventually melded into the faces and bodies of people she had once counted among her friends. But they provided no protection, no barrier, when it came to Jefferson. It was as if there was an alarm system within her that was activated each time he'd look her way. She consciously tried not to think about it.

Yet she could think of hardly anything else.

The tension left her shoulders by degrees. The headache loosened its tentative hold and dissolved into the mists, leaving her free. She talked, she listened. Laughter, she discovered, seemed to come a little easier to her than it had in the past few years. There seemed to be no need for the guard that she always kept up around her. Not here.

Or, at least, not at the moment, she thought, glancing toward Jeff.

When their eyes met and held for an endless moment, it was she who looked away first. It was a lot easier dealing with everyone else in the room than with him, even at a distance. There were too many feelings in the way, too many roads not taken.

And one very important road that had.

Within half an hour, she was eagerly asking questions of her own, catching up on the lives of people she had thought she had put behind her. In her former neighbors' presence, Carole Anne quickly realized that despite everything she had told herself, there was a part of her that was hungry for this kind of information, this kind of contact with the past.

Curiosity, nothing more. A purely reflexive, human reaction. People had a tendency to want to know things, to hear stories finished, mysteries cleared up, the last page of a book being read. She was no different from everyone else in that respect.

Except, she reminded herself as she sipped her punch and carelessly scanned the faces around her over the rim of her glass, she had made it in the outside world while all those here had opted to stay behind.

In the middle of a recitation of her childhood best friend's harrowing first delivery, Carole Anne realized that she hadn't seen Brandon in quite some time. She immediately visualized him standing in a corner of the room, looking on with quiet, sad eyes. A shaft of guilt at her unintentional neglect pierced right through her so sharply she was surprised that she didn't gasp.

Making an excuse, she slipped out of the circle and went to look for her son. She had last seen her aunt guiding Brandon toward a small gathering of children near the porch. But when Carole Anne approached the children, she could see that he wasn't with them.

It didn't surprise her, really. Brandon had a hard time forming relationships. He was happier playing with action toys and spinning stories for his own amusement and hers than interacting with children his own age. He was naturally more comfortable with adults and it worried her at times.

When questioned, none of the children had taken any note of Brandon's absence.

All right, where could he have gotten to? she wondered, looking around.

"Anything wrong?" Emmett asked, coming up behind her.

She turned, a rueful smile on her lips. "I can't find Brandon." She could see by the look in his eyes that the man thought she was overreacting and being more than a little overprotective.

Emmett judiciously kept his comments to himself. "I think I saw him wandering toward the hall a few minutes ago." He pointed toward the doorway. "If you like, I'll help you look."

She shook her head. "No, that's fine. I'm sure he just wandered off." She backed away, then turned toward the doorway.

The sound of Brandon's childish voice grew stronger as she entered the hall. She found him sitting on the stairs, deeply entrenched in a conversation revolving around the latest installment of a favorite comic strip hero. His words were addressed to Jeff.

Carole Anne leaned a hip against the doorjamb, taking it all in. Jeff, she observed, looking perfectly at ease conversing with the child. He wasn't talking down to the boy and he didn't look as if his mind was drifting off as Brandon spoke. Instead he seemed to have found some common level where they could both reside comfortably.

An unbidden pang nudged the pit of her stomach as she watched the scene. She wondered if Jeff was married and had children of his own. No, Aunt Connie would have written to her about it if he had—or would she? She knew that Aunt Connie, in her fluttery, noncommittal sort of way, had always thought they belonged together and had been hurt when Carole Anne ran off with Cal.

When Carole Anne had later admitted that leaving with Cal had been a mistake, Aunt Connie had been placated. She never mentioned Jeff's private life in any of her letters, and Carole Anne couldn't bring herself to ever ask. She had designated a place for Jeff in her past, not her present. It was where he belonged, as did Belle's Grove.

Clearing her throat, she came forward. She was about to drop down onto the bottom step, just below Brandon and Jeff, then thought better of it. She stood on the other side of the banister, keeping the darkly stained wood between her and Jeff.

She looked down at her son. "I thought Aunt Connie was going to introduce you to children your own age."

Brandon looked up at her, startled, as if he hadn't expected her to come by for hours and hours. "Yeah, but they were just kids."

Carole Anne suppressed a smile. "At six, you're not exactly an old man."

"Six and three-quarters," Brandon corrected patiently, slanting a look toward Dr. Jeff to see if that made any difference to the man. He was pleased to see that it seemed to make no impression at all. Brandon jerked a thumb toward his newfound friend. "Dr. Jeff reads 'The Gallant Force' every day, just like I do."

Now that was something she doubted. For one, she didn't think the Belle's Grove *Gazette* carried that strip, or any strip for that matter. It hadn't when she had lived here. Besides, he wasn't the type to read comic strips. They were too frivolous and he too serious to ever successfully mingle.

"Wouldn't miss it," Jeff testified solemnly, his expression never betraying him. "Sgt. Howell's my favorite."

Brandon grinned, his head bobbing up and down emphatically. "Mine, too."

Carole Anne crossed her arms before her and gave Jeff a skeptical look. Maybe he *did* read it. "Small world."

The smile on his rugged face was guileless. "That's what I always said."

And what I chafed against, she thought, remembering. Belle's Grove had felt too small for her, constricting her breathing like a wool sweater that had been accidentally tossed in the dryer. It had made her yearn for an urban world of posh restaurants, theaters and shopping malls that offered a potpourri of merchandise for her to choose from, instead of the same unimaginative selections.

"Dr. Jeff's going to teach me how to fish," Brandon told her excitedly. He liked being around grown-ups. Liked it even more when he wasn't just on the outside, being tolerated, but regarded on a one-to-one basis, the way he was with his mom. And now Dr. Jeff.

Carole Anne frowned. Jeff was making plans for her and she didn't want that. "There isn't time, Brandon," she reminded her son gently.

Jeff moved his shoulders in a careless, habitual motion. "It's not time-consuming," he drawled. "Just needs an afternoon."

Nope, she wasn't going to get caught up in that laid-back, easygoing charm. She all but expected him to add "Aw, shucks." But she wasn't buying into it. Not even a penny's worth. She knew how shrewd a mind there was beneath the surface.

"You don't have to," Carole Anne said pointedly.

"I know." Jeff wondered why she was putting up such a struggle. "It's a matter of wanting to."

He turned toward Brandon and resisted the urge to ruffle the boy's hair. In his opinion, Carole Anne kept her son much too neat. Boys had a need to be boys, and that usually included dirt. That most definitely didn't include jackets. At least not ones worn for more than a few minutes. "Tomorrow?"

Brandon nearly hopped up and down on the step, wishing tomorrow was already here. "Sure!"

Brandon had never been fishing before. And he wasn't that strong a swimmer. What if he fell in? "Brandon, I don't think that's wise—" she began.

His mother's tone had some of the air leaving his balloon. Brandon hesitated, thinking of being alone with a stranger, away from his mother for an entire afternoon. Still, he didn't really want to let this chance go by, either.

Brandon looked hopefully at Jefferson. "Can my mom come, too, Dr. Jeff?"

Jeff heard the uneasiness swell in Brandon's voice. He definitely needed to cut loose a few bonds before it was too late and he grew up into a timid, lackluster soul, grounded in only reality, unable to look at the stars and see something beyond points of light.

Jeff turned innocent green eyes toward Carole Anne. "If she wants to."

Just what was he up to? She could have sworn that there was a gleam there, one she didn't recall ever seeing before. She laced her fingers together around the top of the banister. "Now I know it isn't wise—"

Amusement quirked his mouth. She *was* afraid. But of what? Of him? That was impossible. Of herself? An interesting concept, one he meant to explore. "Why? You used to go fishing all the time."

Yes, a hundred years ago, when she had been too young to know that there was a life out there that was more exciting, more vibrant, than placing worms on a hook and spending the entire day talking and dozing.

"Only until I was fourteen."

"Fifteen," Jeff corrected with a grin. He leaned forward, his eyes keen, daring her. "What's the matter, lose the knack in California?"

Before she could answer, Brandon was on his feet, tugging at her arm. "Please, Mom?"

She could never resist those blue eyes when he pleaded like that. He really did ask for very little for a boy his age. "Oh, all right," she sighed, surrendering. It was just a little outing, what could it hurt? And it was for Brandon, not herself that she was doing it. That made it safe.

She saw satisfaction entering Jeff's eyes and put a condition on her terms. "That is, if Aunt Connie doesn't need me—"

"Aunt Connie will always need you, child." Aunt Connie came up behind her, placing her hands on Carole Anne's shoulders. The girl was stiff as a board. Connie looked from

Jefferson to her niece. This was going to take more prodding than she had initially thought. Carole Anne always was such a stubborn child. Just the way her father had been before her.

Brandon swung toward Aunt Connie, instinctively knowing that here was an ally. "Dr. Jeff asked me—us—to go fishing."

Aunt Connie nodded her approval. About time Jefferson mended that fence of his, letting Carole Anne get away like that. Terrible waste. Made a body lose faith in the path of true love.

"Wonderful." She took Brandon's hand in hers. "I could use some trout," she told him, as if she was placing an order at the seafood counter at the local supermarket.

Carole Anne felt as if she was standing in the path of an oncoming snowball that was quickly turning into boulder proportions. "Aunt Connie, I thought you said you needed me."

"Not twenty-four hours a day, child." Aunt Connie laughed away the notion. "I'm seventy-three, child, not two. And I do have some of my faculties left."

Of that, Carole Anne was sure. Perhaps even more faculties than she had given the older woman credit for. This was beginning to smell suspiciously like a setup.

"And now," Aunt Connie cheerfully chirped, "if you don't mind, I'm borrowing Brandon again. I need some help in the kitchen."

If anyone was leaving the area, it was going to be her, not Brandon. Carole Anne placed a hand on her aunt's arm. "I can—"

"No," Aunt Connie said firmly, "you can't. This is a little boy detail."

Soft brows puckered, forming a wavy, indignant line over his blue eyes. "I'm not a little boy," Brandon informed Aunt Connie.

"He's six and three-quarters," Jeff put in as an explanation. He exchanged a conspiratorial grin with Brandon.

"Close enough," Aunt Connie pronounced solemnly. With that, she led Brandon away.

Because she felt awkward just standing there, Carole Anne sat down on the last step, though she avoided Jeff's eyes. She laced her hands around her knees, tucking her skirt around them primly first. Jeff caught the movement and smiled to himself. "Not very subtle, is she?"

"Works for me." Jeff grinned. "She'll do."

He took a breath. There was so much he wanted to say. He didn't know where to begin. The words were all tangled up in a giant skein of emotions within his soul. All he knew was that he had to start slowly to keep from frightening her off, the way he had once done before. He settled for the most obvious topic.

"He's a handsome boy." He looked down into her face, his eyes pinning her, absorbing every nuance beneath hooded lashes. "Looks like Cal, as I remember."

She laced her fingers tighter, dropping them into her lap. She sat very still. The noise of the party behind her faded in her ears like the cry of a bird as it flew into the distance. "Yes, I know."

He wanted to reach out to her, to hold her, to shake her for hurting him. To kiss her because until he had seen her walk through that door today, he hadn't fully comprehended just how much he had missed her. "Why did he leave you, Carole Anne?"

She looked up at him sharply. No one was supposed to know about that. She had strived to make sure people believed it had been a mutually agreed upon divorce, not something so devastating as discovering herself abandoned one morning with a note in her hand.

"Aunt Connie?" she guessed. Her voice wavered between an accusation and disappointment. But then, she knew that words were her aunt's constant companion and she liked to share them on a regular basis. Aunt Connie considered the immediate world her friend. And Jeff was part of the immediate world.

"Aunt Connie," he confirmed.

If she told him that, she probably told him the rest of it, as well. Carole Anne shrugged, turning away. "Then you know."

"No. I haven't a clue." He had thought Cal Wellsley out of his mind when he had learned that the man had abandoned Carole Anne. Some people never knew when they were well off. "I only know that I wouldn't have."

She shut out his last words. She didn't want to think of that, didn't want to think of the path not taken.

"Peter Pan probably had something to do with it." She saw Jeff looking at her questioningly. "Cal didn't want to grow up. He just wanted to have fun, to be free." She sighed, remembering. "Endless rides on the merry-go-round without ever having to pay the price of a ticket."

She turned and looked off in the direction that Aunt Connie had taken Brandon. She missed seeing Jeff clench his fists. "When I got pregnant, I knew it was time to get off, and I did. Cal didn't. It was almost as if he couldn't. He decided that being a husband and father wasn't what he wanted to do with his life." She looked down at her hand. She had taken the ring off more than five years ago. At times, it still felt as if it were there.

Jeff knew those kinds of things happened all the time, but he still couldn't understand abandoning someone like that. Especially if that someone was Carole Anne. "You haven't heard from him?"

For a moment, Carole Anne thought he was going to reach out to her, and she shifted, shaking her head. She didn't want his pity. "After a while, I stopped wanting to. I had Brandon and then a career. My life's full." The defiant look in her eyes dared him to argue with her. "So how's yours?"

He thought of the long hours, the clinic filled to bursting. The frustration over the conditions he couldn't cure. The elation when he could. He smiled. It could all be summed up in one word. "Busy."

Just as short-winded as ever. Some things didn't change, she thought. "You stayed here just like you said you would."

Yes, but you were supposed to stay with me. "Doc Williams retired." He lifted his shoulders and let them fall in a careless shrug, as if there had never been an alternate plan. He was destined to be a doctor here, where he grew up. Where people needed him. "Someone had to take over."

But it didn't have to be you. Why didn't you want to be brave and go out, see what you could accomplish? Why did you have feet of clay? The words throbbed in her throat, but she left them unsaid. "Still a one-doctor town?"

Did she realize that there was a hint of condescension in her voice? Probably not. He nodded. "That's all that's necessary. Anything really serious comes up, I send them to the county hospital in the next town." He let his eyes roam over her hair and remembered tucking daisies into it. A crown of flowers he had made her that day. "I just stick bandages on people."

"You do a lot more than that, according to Aunt Connie."

He didn't want to waste time talking about himself. "Aunt Connie tends to exaggerate. For instance, she told me you were very happy." He leaned forward. "Or so you wrote."

She raised her chin defensively. She wasn't going to let him analyze her. "I *am* happy."

"Your eyes aren't." It was the first thing he had noticed.

She looked away. Damn him for prying. "That's just irritation from the smog."

Let her have her lie for the time being. There was time enough later for truth. "Missouri air'll cure that fast enough," he said easily.

Her back stiffened. "I don't intend to be here that long. Just until the wedding." She looked toward the parlor. Emmett seemed to stand out above the crowd. He was laughing and talking to someone she didn't recognize. A confederate? "If it comes off."

Jeff followed her gaze and saw nothing unusual. "What do you mean?"

Time to get down to business. She turned to face him again. "What do you know about Emmett Carson? I couldn't get any information out of Aunt Connie when I asked. We never seemed to get past how wonderful he was. What does he do? Is he retired?" Myriad questions flooded her mind.

He grinned at her suspicious tone. Only someone who didn't know the man would be so wary. "That's right, you left before he moved here."

He made it sound like a crime, even though there was no change in his voice or in his expression. She could *feel* his accusation. She'd known Jeff since the time she was able to form memories, and that was definitely an accusation in his voice.

She worked her way past it. "So, what do you know about him?" Aunt Connie had said he was younger than she was—by six years. That put him around retirement age. "Does he work?"

He wondered if she knew that she was making noises as if she was Aunt Connie's mother instead of her niece. "Occasionally."

"Where?"

"The bank?"

Embezzlement. The word jumped up at her in red-rimmed letters. "Occasionally?" she questioned, probing.

"What exactly does he do there?" Maybe he was the security guard there.

"Runs it, mostly."

"Excuse me?"

He watched her eyes as he told her. Amazement had always made her eyes grow, like a child's eyes watching it snow for the first time. "He's the bank president. I put him on a reduced schedule last spring. He had a heart attack. A very minor heart attack," he stressed when he saw the look of alarm rise in her eyes. "If you're worried that he's after Aunt Connie's money, don't be. If I didn't know him, I would have checked him out myself."

He made her feel as if she had been remiss about a lot of things. She stonewalled the feeling. "Why?"

Was it so hard for her to understand? "Because I care about Aunt Connie. I care about a lot of people in this town."

Carole Anne pressed her lips together, pushing memories away with both hands. They kept coming, like a river swelling during a flood. "I remember. The good samaritan."

"You make it sound like a failing," he said evenly.

She hadn't wanted to put it that bluntly. "No, it's just that—"

"Good is boring?" he guessed, reading her mind.

She rose, drawing herself up. "Don't put words into my mouth."

"Fine, then you put words there." Jeff reached up and caught her by the wrist. "Help me understand, Carole Anne."

She pulled her hand free. Something entirely too distracting was happening when he held it.

"There's nothing to understand." She turned and began to walk away. Quickly. "Excuse me, I have some catching up to do."

"And so do I, Carole Anne," Jefferson said softly as he watched her go. "So do I."

Chapter Three

Connie sighed happily as she began to unload her dishwasher. "It was a lovely party, wasn't it, Carole Anne?"

"Lovely," Carole Anne echoed.

There was nervous energy humming through her veins. She'd felt it ever since she had walked through the door. Ever since she had seen Jeff. Maybe she was just overtired, she reasoned.

Or was she just rationalizing? she thought disparagingly as she picked up a dish towel with a dancing dairymaid embroidered on it. Embroidering was Aunt Connie's passion, she recalled fondly as she began to rub a glass clear of water spots.

Overtired or not, she *was* overreacting, she upbraided herself. What *was* it that she was afraid of?

"But you shouldn't have gone to that much trouble," she told her aunt.

Connie frowned at the protest as well as at another water spot. She looked at Carole Anne over the glass she was holding, mild surprise in her eyes at her niece's statement.

"These were your friends and mine, and you're my niece. There was no trouble involved." Connie narrowed her eyes, staring at Carole Anne as if the younger woman was being just the slightest bit addle-brained about the situation. "I love doing this."

She turned from the dishwasher to find Brandon next to her. He was holding a stack of dessert dishes that had been overlooked in the living room. Connie took them from him.

"Thank you, dear." Connie smiled over the boy's head at her niece. "You've done a very fine job of raising him, Carole Anne." Her expressive face puckered in sympathy. "Such a shame you had to do it alone."

Carole Anne had a feeling she knew what was coming. She lifted a shoulder carelessly and let it drop. "For the most part, you raised me all by yourself and I don't think you did such a bad job, either. Besides, it's not the number of parents, Aunt Connie, it's the love. You used to tell me that all the time, remember?"

She realized that she had been rubbing the same spot now for more than two minutes and set the glass aside.

Connie picked up the glass and placed it into the cupboard. Thinking the step stool too much trouble, the older woman tottered on her toes to reach the shelf.

"Yes, I did, and it's true, you turned out very well. Still..." Her voice trailed off meaningfully.

Taller than her aunt by five inches, Carole Anne put the next two glasses into the cupboard herself. It was time to change direction before Connie started driving down a road Carole Anne had no intentions of traveling.

"About Emmett, Aunt Connie," she began.

At the mention of her fiancé's name, a smile blossomed on Connie's face as quickly as daisies bloomed in the spring. She clasped her hands together joyously, like a heroine in an old-fashioned melodrama. "Isn't he just wonderful?"

So everyone at the party seemed to feel. Carole Anne was more than happy to take that as a testimonial. But life had made her very wary, robbing her of an optimism that she had only partially owned to begin with. She would have died rather than see her aunt hurt.

"Yes, well, I think we need to sit down and have a talk."

Carole Anne glanced at Brandon. He was sitting at the kitchen table, nibbling away at the frosting on the last piece of the cake. It brought back fond memories of her own childhood, when she had sat at this very table, sampling wondrous confections that emerged out of Aunt Connie's magic oven.

This wasn't the time or the place to begin a friendly investigation.

"Soon," she added.

Connie turned from the dishwasher, a fistful of silverware in her hand. She smiled benevolently at Carole Anne as she patted her niece's hand.

"Thank you, but there's really no need for a talk, dear. I *have* been married before, you know." Connie opened the drawer and began to sort out the silverware, dropping them into their respective spaces. She sighed. Carole Anne could have sworn it was wistfully. "Though it was a very long time ago, I do imagine things are still done the same."

She looked over her shoulder at Carole Anne. A blush, pink and fresh, rose up her translucent cheeks like the first carnations in the spring. But her eyes were sparkling with anticipation.

Carole Anne laughed as she shook her head. "That's not the kind of talk I had in mind."

Satisfied that all the dishes, except for the ones that Brandon had found, were put away, Connie closed the dishwasher door and wiped her hands. She looked at Carole Anne with mild interest.

"What did you have in mind, dear?"

Perhaps now *was* the time. Carole Anne sat down at the table next to Brandon and motioned for her aunt to join her. Connie eased herself into the chair and waited patiently.

Carole Anne took a deep breath and dove in. "What do you know about Emmett?"

Connie's smile was tolerant, as if she was dealing with a slow-witted offspring. "Everything I need to know, dear. He makes me happy." Remembering something else she had to do, Connie was on her feet again.

This was not going well. Carole Anne was getting the impression that Aunt Connie was entering into a lifelong commitment with apparently less thought than she gave to purchasing a new pair of shoes.

She caught Aunt Connie's arm before the woman had a chance to cross to the stove. "But—"

Connie laid a comforting hand on top of Carole Anne's. "At my age, dear, there isn't much room for 'buts.' I have to take my happiness where I find it and quickly because it might not happen again. Actually—" she rolled the thought over slowly in her mind as she hung up her towel "—that might be said at any age." She fixed Carole Anne with a motherly look. "Now, Jeff—"

Time to retreat. Carole Anne pushed away from the table. "Jeff will be coming to take Brandon fishing tomorrow, so I'd better get him to bed." She hustled Brandon to his feet. Brandon took one final, quick lick of the frosting. "This is way past his bedtime."

"Jeff is taking you, too," Connie reminded her. There was an anticipatory look in her eyes that made Carole Anne uneasy.

She shrugged a bit too casually as she placed her hands on Brandon's shoulders. "We'll see," Carole Anne murmured. In the morning, she'd find a way to get out of the situation. Brandon would be too excited to notice that she wasn't coming along.

Brandon twisted around to look at his mother. "Please, Mom, you promised."

So much for him not noticing.

"Yes, I did." She looked down at Brandon. His cheeks looked flushed, as flushed as her aunt's had a few moments ago. Carole Anne cupped Brandon's chin in her hand and studied him carefully. "Are you feeling all right, honey?"

Brandon pulled back, embarrassed by the fuss, and then yawned. "Sleepy," he murmured.

Connie gently elbowed Carole Anne out of the way and took her turn looking the little boy over. She smiled kindly at him.

"It's probably just all the excitement," she pronounced. "And maybe a few too many cookies." She beamed. Connie loved a healthy appetite. "He'll be fine in the morning."

Well, her son might be fine in the morning, Carole Anne thought, but she wouldn't be. Not if she didn't get any sleep. It was past midnight and she was still awake. She bunched up her pillow and sighed.

Lying in the bed where she had spun so many dreams while she was growing up, Carole Anne couldn't sleep. It was as if there were ghosts from her past waiting for her in this room, making her remember, filling her with nostalgia.

When she'd first entered the room, she'd been surprised and perhaps a little pleased to discover that Aunt Connie hadn't changed anything. Apparently all she had ever done was dust here. Her bedroom was exactly the way she had left it that morning she had run off, except that the bed had been made, she noted with a rueful smile. She had almost cried when she saw it. It was a room that belonged to a girl with grandiose dreams. Dreams that didn't include a little town like Belle's Grove.

Now as Carole Anne lay in bed, watching shadows dance through the outline of the branches cast by the tree outside her window, memories were crowding her mind like cars jamming onto a freeway at rush hour. She wanted to shut them out, but they refused to leave. Instead they were taking her back, making her remember that it hadn't all been so terrible, so constricting, living here. With the gift of hindsight, she could see that her life, all in all, had been one filled with love and security.

And that had been due to Aunt Connie. And perhaps, just a tad, because of Jeff.

She didn't want to think of Jeff.

Because she didn't, like a perverse gremlin, her mind proceeded to conjure up *only* memories of Jeff. A panorama of bits and pieces of reminiscences of her past, all involving Jeff, meandered through her head.

Carole Anne couldn't specifically remember the first time she had ever seen him. There had to have been a first time, but for the life of her, she couldn't recall. It seemed as if he had always been part of her life. He lived about a quarter of a mile away from her aunt's house, which made them almost next door neighbors. They were both without siblings. Jeff gradually became her unofficial older brother, keeping an eye on her, sometimes with almost maddening protectiveness.

Two years ahead of her at school, he had been tall, shy, and really terribly sweet. "As steadfast as a tree," Aunt Connie had been fond of saying. And at times, Carole Anne thought, smiling into the night, about as communicative as one.

But he had always been there for her. They first found common ground in the fact that she was an orphan and he was fatherless. They had grown up together, sharing heartaches, secrets and dreams. Jeff had always seemed older than his years, more serious than the other boys his age. Maybe he had to be, she thought now, looking back. He had taken on being the man in his family at an early age, feeling responsible for his mother. Jeff had *always* felt responsible for people, Carole Anne remembered, recalling how he had taken her under his wing.

Carole Anne shut her eyes tight and prayed for rain.

The sky was a crystal clear shade of icy blue as it poked its way into her room, pushing sunbeams through the crack in her curtain and running them along the floor like heralds announcing the arrival of a king.

Carole Anne dragged herself out of the comalike sleep that had finally enveloped her and sat up. She didn't have to look into the mirror to know that she looked half dead. She had never been a morning person. Morning was something that came crashing in on her like a marauding enemy. It attacked her slumber, robbing her of it while forcing her to face the world when all she wanted to do was bury her head in a pillow for a few more hours.

But it was time to bear up to the inevitable. Morning was here and so, no doubt, was Jeff, or soon would be. She vaguely recalled that he thrived on mornings.

The man was obviously sick.

Dragging on a pink terry-cloth bathrobe that was long on comfort and short on style, Carole Anne stumbled down the back stairs, led by her nose. Aunt Connie's coffee always was alluring.

But it wasn't Aunt Connie whom she saw first when she entered the sunny, wide country kitchen. Jefferson Drumm was perched on a stool by the breakfast nook. He was nursing a cup of coffee and nibbling at a doughnut as if he had just as much right to be there as the assorted mugs hanging from the rack on the counter.

Damn, she thought she would have had at least a few minutes to pull herself together before she had to face him. She might have known he wouldn't stand on ceremony.

Trying her best to be civil, Carole Anne dragged a hand through a tangle of blond hair and attempted to clear her mind of the cobwebs of sleep that still clung there.

"Good morning, dear, did you sleep well?" Without missing a beat, Connie moved to the coffeepot to pour a cup for Carole Anne. In her other hand she held a spatula and expertly flipped another four pancakes over on the grill. They moved like syncopated dancers in a water ballet, landing one after the other.

"So-so. I always have trouble sleeping in a new bed." She realized the mistake in her wording by the look on her aunt's face. "I mean, other than the one I'm used to in L.A."

Fumbling, she turned her bleary eyes on Jeff and struggled to focus. The man looked like a fixture. A very relaxed fixture. "What are you doing here?"

He raised his mug as if to toast her. "We have a date to go fishing, remember?"

Carole Anne gratefully accepted the mug that Connie handed her. Clutching it in both hands, she closed her eyes and took a long sip of the black liquid. She didn't speak as she absorbed the sensation of the coffee pouring itself through her body to her stomach, nudging all parts of her fully awake.

When she opened her eyes, she found that Jeff was studying her. And smiling broadly. She remembered that smile. It was the one that could charm birds out of trees. It was shy, beguiling and sexy all at the same time.

Why *wasn't* he married by now? Were all the women in Belle's Grove slow-witted? No, not that she could recall. She wondered if he had turned into one of those people married to their work.

"We don't," she finally mumbled into her mug. "You and Brandon do."

Jeff set his mug down. No sooner did the bottom touch the counter than Aunt Connie was refilling it, beaming at him as if he was a national treasure she had uncovered all on her own.

He shook his head in reply to Carole Anne's words. "No, it's the three of us, all right." He indicated Connie with his mug. "I have a witness."

Connie looked at her niece and nodded solemnly as she replaced the coffeepot.

"Sold out by my own flesh and blood." Carole Anne sighed dramatically, resigned. She glanced down at the robe as if she hadn't noticed it before. "I guess I'd better get dressed then."

His grin widened, doing strange things to her nervous system. Tiny pieces of his smile were weaving their way under her skin, warming it. "Unless you want to flash the fish."

She sniffed, pulling her sash tighter. "I'll have you know I'm wearing a nightgown underneath."

His eyes trailed slowly up and down the length of her body, making Carole Anne feel as if she was wearing translucent black lace instead of durable terry cloth.

"A pity," he commented.

This time, the smile hit her like a B12 injection, completely startling her.

Slightly disoriented and unnerved by the very blatant, basic reaction she was having to Jeff, Carole Anne decided that in this case, retreat was the better part of valor. She turned on her heel and moved toward the back stairs, still clutching her mug, more for support than for anything else.

"I'll, um, be right back," she muttered.

Jeff got off the stool and brought his dish to the sink. "If you're not down in fifteen minutes, I'm coming up for you," he called up the back stairs after her.

In the distance, Carole Anne heard her aunt attempting to force a stack of pancakes on Jeff. She couldn't help feeling as if she was in the midst of a conspiracy.

"It's not going to work," she told her absent aunt. One time on the merry-go-round was enough for her. Cal had cured her permanently of foolish dreams. She had more important things on her mind than romance and paths not taken. She had a son and a career and that was more than enough for her.

Fifteen minutes later, Carole Anne returned to the kitchen. She was just buttoning her last button as she looked around.

"Where's Brandon?" She hadn't bothered checking on him while she was upstairs because she had just assumed that he had already flown down the stairs, raring to go.

"Why, I thought he'd be coming down with you, dear," Connie said, wiping her hands on her apron.

"It's not like him to sleep in." Carole Anne glanced up, as if she could see her son through the ceiling. "I'll just go back up and—"

Jeff took the opportunity to push aside his half-empty plate. Connie was an excellent cook and since she had taken over the job of mothering him, he had had to exercise twice as rigorously to keep from moving his belt over a full notch.

"Why don't we both go up?" Jeff suggested as he took her elbow.

Basic survival instinct, honed because of Cal, had her pulling her elbow away. Carole Anne didn't want Jeff intruding into her life like this. Even the smallest amount. She wanted no doors opening that she had shut once. "He's my son."

If there was offense to be taken at her annoyed tone, Jeff didn't seem aware of it. He was already ahead of her on the stairs. "Yes, but he's my fishing partner."

Carole Anne had to hurry to keep up. There he went again, taking charge, she thought, assuming things he had no right to assume. Fishing partner, her foot.

She elbowed him out of her way and opened the door to Brandon's room. Behind them she could hear Aunt Connie bringing up the rear.

When she walked into the room, she found Brandon sitting on his bed. He was only partially dressed, with his shirt haphazardly hanging open. One sock was held listlessly in his hand while the other was on his foot, bunched up at the toe.

The first thing Carole Anne noticed was that Brandon's eyes looked glazed and liquidy. Concerned, she rushed over to him. "Oh, honey, you're sick."

Brandon tried to shake his head vehemently, but the effort was obviously too much for him. His cheeks were hot blotches of pink, like stove elements about to go on high. He looked absolutely miserable.

"I'm not sick," he protested with as much feeling as he could muster.

Carole Anne felt his forehead. She didn't need a thermometer to verify that he was running a fever. "Oh, yes, you are."

Brandon turned runny blue eyes toward Jeff. "But I'm going fishing today." He bit his lower lip to keep from crying. Men didn't cry, and his mother called him her big man. He didn't want Dr. Jeff to think he was a baby.

Jeff laid a sympathetic hand on the boy's shoulder. "I'm afraid I have some bad news."

Brandon's lower lip was out, pouting. He thought Dr. Jeff was going to be different. Not like those others who his mother saw. They only talked nicely to him when they thought they were impressing his mother. Brandon's shoulders slumped and he gave up trying to be brave. "You can't take me?"

Casually, Jeff brushed his fingers along the column of the boy's throat. Glands swollen. Runny nose. Eyes glazed. Probably just a simple cold. Just as casually, Jeff squatted to Brandon's level.

"Not today, I'm afraid. I forgot that today's the day they clean the lake." He watched, amused, as Brandon's eyes opened wide. "We like to keep our waters clean here in Missouri," he explained to the boy. "But they say that the lake'll be ready for fishing in a couple of days. Possibly even as early as tomorrow." He gave the boy's shoulder a conspiratorial pat. "Think you can be better by then?"

Brandon nodded his head. The dark hair fell into his eyes and he moved back as his mother brushed it out of his eyes. He looked up at Jeff. "Sure."

Carole Anne was already tugging off his other sock. "In that case, I think that you'd better get back into bed, young man."

He didn't want to be in bed. He wanted to be where things were happening. "But—"

It had been a long time since Connie had heard that sad, protesting tone. Not since Carole Anne had been little. She gently moved Jeff aside and sat down on the bed next to Brandon.

"You know, I haven't had a little person to read to in such a long time." Connie sighed wistfully as she placed her arm around Brandon's small shoulders. "Do you like stories, Brandon?"

He was about to protest that he wasn't a "little person," but the offer interested him. He cocked his head. "With bad guys?"

Aunt Connie drew her brows together to look as fierce as she could for his benefit. "The baddest."

Brandon managed a hoarse giggle. "Sure."

Knuckles digging onto the comforter, Connie rose to her feet. She struck a bargain, one she had struck many times before when Carole Anne had been Brandon's age. "You get into bed and I'll come back in fifteen minutes with a story that'll make your eyes pop out. And I just happen to have a batch of fresh chocolate-chip cookies."

"For breakfast?" Carole Anne protested. A strong sense of nutrition had replaced what had once been a rather ravenous sweet tooth.

Connie appeared woefully disappointed in her niece's lack of compassion. The girl obviously had been gone too long.

"The boy's sick. He deserves to be pampered a little." Connie turned toward Jeff, whom she regarded as a higher authority. "Right?"

Jeff kept a solemn expression on his face. "I can write a prescription to that effect."

Carole Anne threw up her hands. She supposed that one day wouldn't matter that much. "I guess I know when I'm outnumbered."

Jeff took her arm and ushered her from the room. "I certainly hope so." Before she could ask him just what he thought he was up to, Jeff was guiding her toward the back stairs.

He looked at the simple white shorts and halter top. "I didn't get a chance to tell you that you look pretty sexy for a fishing trip."

She stopped on the bottom step and stared at him. He was talking as if they were still going. "What fishing trip?"

"The one we're going on," he answered matter-of-factly. "You don't expect the fish to come to us."

"I don't expect anything at all. We're not going on one now." Wondering how he had managed to maneuver her down the stairs without her fully realizing it, she began to retrace her steps, but he stopped her.

"We're not? Why?"

She didn't like standing so close to him. The stairwell was narrow and much too confining. There was hardly room for two people to stand next to one another. She knew it was silly, but she felt as if something was happening to her, as if she was standing on the ledge of a precipice, waiting for it to break off and send her plummeting into a bottomless pit.

"Because Brandon's not coming."

He shrugged as if what she was saying made no sense. "So you'll break in his pole for him."

Why was he being so dense? He was a doctor, wasn't he? "He's sick. He needs me."

"He has a cold, Carole Anne," Jeff said patiently, still holding on to her arm. "You can't make him get over it and Aunt Connie's going to be here reading to him. We're not leaving him alone in the throes of pneumonia." He smiled into her eyes. "Any more excuses?"

Her resistance seemed to evaporate. Maybe it would be fun at that. She meant to take in the lake before she left Belle's Grove. She had spent many happy hours there, daydreaming. And fishing with Jeff.

"I can't think of any right now." She took another step up. "Just give me a minute—"

He knew better than to let her escape. "No, I've already given you too many minutes as it is. Let's go." He gently tugged on her arm. "The fish like to get up early around here."

She bit her lower lip, torn as she glanced up the stairs. "But what'll I tell Brandon?"

That was easy. "That we're going to check on the people cleaning the lake for him."

He liked the fact that she was so concerned about her son, but at the same time, he knew she had to give the boy a little slack. Nothing thrived and grew under smothering conditions.

Carole Anne didn't like it. "I've never lied to him before."

She saw things too black and white, he thought. He had learned to find shades of gray and beige. It was the only way to survive. "You'd rather let him think he's missing out on going fishing?"

He was making her sound heartless. "Well, no, but lying to him—"

Taking her hand, Jeff guided her into the kitchen. "Creative fabrication," he informed her, pressing both hands to her back to move her farther along, "is the only way to spare feelings. Tell you what, I'll go and tell him, you pack some sandwiches."

Carole Anne gave a short laugh as she fisted hands on her waist. "I have to feed you, too?"

He grinned. "Small price to pay for a morning of fishing with Belle's Grove's only physician and most eligible bachelor."

She cocked her head and studied him, as if that would help answer her question. It didn't. It only compounded it. "Why are you?"

The urge to kiss her pumped through him, hard and urgent. He ignored it. For now. She was asking him a question. "Most eligible? Town has low standards, I guess."

She shook her head. Her question was more basic than that. "A bachelor."

He smiled, amused.

Carole Anne felt that strange zing traveling through her again. This time she felt as if she was a guitar string that had just been plucked. It was a moment before she ceased vibrating.

Though he was smiling, his voice was serious when he answered. "Because I never found anyone who could compare to you."

Uh-oh. Time to bail out. Fast. Carole Anne took a step backward. "Jeff, maybe I had better not—"

He shook his head, cutting her protest short. He had been too passive in the past. That was where his trouble lay. If he hadn't been so easygoing, so undemanding, he would have been the one exchanging vows with Carole Anne, not Cal.

But he had been given a fresh opportunity now. He wasn't about to waste it. This time the lady wasn't going to slip through his fingers. He placed his hands on her shoulders as she began to move away.

"No, maybe you better had." Slowly he slid his hands down her arms until he finally let them drop to his sides. Just touching her had him remembering. And longing. He grinned. "I'll just confer with my patient and be back in five minutes. Start spreading mayonnaise on some bread."

There was something in his eyes she couldn't remember having seen before. Determination. A power that had Carole Anne swallowing her protest, at least for now. She barely remembered nodding her head as a shiver slithered up her spine employing the same tempo as his hands had a moment ago. Slow and sexy. And almost bone-melting.

With a twinge of nervous anticipation pinching her stomach, Carole Anne opened the refrigerator to see exactly what Aunt Connie had that might lend itself to a picnic.

Or a final meal at a wake.

Hers.

Chapter Four

It looked just the way she remembered it. Perhaps the water was a little bluer, and the willow trees that surrounded the lake like green royal guardsmen a little taller and shaggier than when she'd last seen them, but basically, it was just the way she remembered it.

Carole Anne stared at the surroundings, unconsciously absorbing them as Jeff brought his pickup truck to a stop a few yards from the edge of the lake.

He sat in the driver's seat patiently waiting for her to open the door. He sensed that she was experiencing a wave of nostalgia and any memories that were wafting through her could only be to his benefit.

She realized that he was watching her. She flushed as she got out, feeling a little foolish for momentarily being carried away. She closed the passenger door and followed Jeff to the back of the truck. "I feel a little guilty being here without Brandon."

Jeff picked up the basket Aunt Connie had provided. Carole Anne had dumped a few hastily wrapped sandwiches and a couple of cans of soda inside. Two of the sandwiches were bursting out of their aluminum foil wrappers even as he closed the lid. He was glad for her sake that she wrote better than she wrapped.

He handed Carole Anne a fishing pole and picked up the other one. Carole Anne looked the rod and reel over. Strictly basic stuff, Carole Anne noted as Jeff led the short distance down to the lake. He dropped the basket under a tree.

"Don't worry." He leaned his pole against the willow. "I'll take Brandon as soon as he's well, which'll probably be tomorrow or the day after that."

She tested her pole's weight in her hand absently. Apparently Jeff had a lot of free time on his hands. Either that, or he was making empty promises. It didn't sound like the Jeff she knew, but then, everyone changed. Look at her. The stars in her eyes had turned out to be merely reflections of harsh neon lights, she thought.

"How can you manage that, being the only doctor in town?"

Taking the pole in his hand, Jeff slid his long frame down onto the ground and propped himself up against the tree. "Not exactly. Sheila's a nurse practitioner."

Carole Anne sat down beside him. It almost seemed like old times. Almost. She wondered who Sheila was, and if she was pretty. "Really? A nurse practitioner here in Belle's Grove?"

Jeff cocked a brow as he set the pole down and looked at her. It was hard to miss the surprise in her voice. He lapsed into a pronounced twang, hooking one thumb through a belt loop. "Yes, by cracky, we got ourselves one of them newfangled nurse prac-tish-ner people."

Embarrassed, Carole Anne blew out a breath. She had that coming to her. She had sounded like one of the very snobs she hated, the people who looked down their noses at her when she mentioned where she came from. "All right, I deserved that."

The sound of Jeff's laugh floated through the morning air, carried by the gentle breeze. The breeze would be gone soon. It was going to be another hot day. The sun already felt strong and it was sifting long golden fingers through her hair, turning it into almost a pale ash. He wanted to run his fingers through it. He wanted to pull her close and just feel her breathing against him.

"We're not backward or primitive here, Carole Anne. Just small. Nothing wrong with being small." He looked at her meaningfully. Unable to resist, he brushed his fingertips along the ends of her hair. "Some of my favorite things are small."

She could feel her stomach tightening again, as if she was on top of a twenty-story roller coaster that split second before it went hurtling down. She wasn't about to go hurtling down, not ever again. She'd learned her lesson. "Don't."

He lingered a beat, then dropped his hand. "Don't what? Touch your hair?" He picked up the fishing pole again. He needed something to do with his hands.

She huffed, upset and not completely certain why. "You know what I mean." She hoped he did because she wasn't sure *what* she meant. She only knew he was stirring things that she didn't want disturbed.

"Don't touch off your guilt?" he guessed. He leaned back a little, his eyes never leaving her face. "I couldn't if there wasn't any."

Her head shot up, a defensive look in her eyes. "I am not guilty."

The smile was slow, lazy and sad. She had no defense against it. She was a screen door attempting to block the smells of a summer barbecue. It permeated her and, like smoke, clung to her. "Yes, you are. You're guilty of robbing us of eight years."

Carole Anne broke eye contact first, afraid that he would see things within her that she wasn't even certain she knew existed. He'd always been able to see right through her.

She stared at the lake. A mother duck was paddling across with five ducklings following her. Carole Anne wished that life was that simple. But it never had been. Not for her.

"You scared me, Jeff," she said softly, almost talking to herself.

He believed her. And it hurt. He had always loved her. How could Carole Anne have been afraid of him? "Scared you? How?"

She clenched her hands at her sides, as if that gave her the strength to speak. "I was just twenty years old. Too young to stagnate here."

Her words stung like the point of a sharp sword. They were more than just an indictment against Belle's Grove. He was *part* of Belle's Grove and, in effect, she had lumped him into the oppressive feelings living here had generated. "I see, too young to settle down with me, but not too young to run off with Cal."

She swung her head around so quickly that her hair glided behind her. "That was different."

"How?" His voice was hoarse with the emotions that rose up in his throat. "How was it different?" Jeff curbed the anger, rough and raw, that threatened to erupt within him, just as it had the day he had heard the news that she was gone.

She lifted her shoulders and let them drop helplessly. "It just was."

He dropped the pole and shifted until he faced her, his hands on her shoulders. "Because Cal was for a blink of an eye and I was forever. And deep down you knew it." He looked at her intently. "And 'forever' frightened you."

Carole Anne struggled to her feet. She wanted to get away from the confrontation, from the hurt, accusing look in his eyes. But Jeff wouldn't let her escape. He stood up. It was time to have it out. The past had to be out in the open if they were to go forward.

And he was determined that they were.

"You were my girl, Carole Anne. Mine. In here." He tapped a finger on the center of his chest, near his heart. When she turned away, he caught her by the shoulders again. "You were mine. Just as much mine as I was yours."

Carole Anne wanted to pull away, but she couldn't. He held her fast, not just imprisoning her arms, but imprisoning her very soul with the look in his eyes.

She tried to make him understand now what she couldn't make him understand then. "Don't you see? I didn't want to stay here. You did. I wanted to try my wings and soar."

He released her. "So, you've soared. Is it as wonderful as you thought?"

No, there were disappointments, at times so overwhelming she didn't think she could bear it. And there were nights when she felt devastatingly alone and lost. But it was all a price she had to pay for growing up. Everyone did in their own way, she thought.

But she couldn't admit that to him. "Yes," she said stubbornly. "It is. I've become someone, made something of myself." Her words gained momentum as she defended her choice. "My marriage didn't work, but my career did. And I have a hell of a son, so it wasn't such a loss, after all." Standing toe-to-toe with him now, the look in her eyes challenged Jeff to dispute her words.

There was fire in her eyes. It made her look magnificent, he thought. He'd never seen her really angry before.

"No, you're right. He is a hell of a kid." Jeff looked out at the peaceful water. The mother duck was still paddling along, her brood following behind. People made life too complicated, he thought. It could really all be very simple if they let it. That was why he liked living in Belle's Grove.

He turned toward her again. His expression softened. "I don't want to argue with you, Carole Anne."

She let out a breath, the momentum of her anger dissipated, surrendering its kinetic energy. "Neither do I. I'm only staying for the wedding. I'd rather not fill that time with words both of us will regret." She had anticipated that coming here with him like this without Brandon would create problems. It had been a bad idea all around. She licked her lips. "Maybe you'd better take me home."

He grinned and the hard feelings that existed between them dissolved. "No, I think that maybe I should bait your hook instead." He nodded at the naked curved iron. "You stand a better chance of catching something if you have a worm on your hook."

His response surprised her. She had thought that perhaps they were better off going their separate ways for the day. "You still want to fish?"

He took the can of worms he had collected from his garden this morning out of the paper sack. "That was the reason we came," he said as he sat down.

She shrugged, settling on the ground beside him. "Okay, but you have to bait my hook."

"I said I would." He took a firm grip of her hook and threaded the worm on it carefully.

Carole Anne shivered and looked away. She'd never been able to do this part. And she didn't even like worms. "How do you reconcile your Hippocratic oath with impaling live worms?"

"They never came into the clinic for treatment." He made certain the worm was securely on, then wiped his hand on the back of his jeans. "There." He handed the pole back to Carole Anne. "All set."

She cast out her line. The hook swished overhead, humming. It created a tiny splash as it landed in the water. Carole Anne leaned against the tree next to Jeff. The moment was almost idyllic. Like everything else here, it brought back memories. "Think we'll catch something?"

He took a deep breath, inhaling her fragrance. It went straight to his bloodstream, drugging him. He shrugged, attempting to seem unfazed.

"A little sun. A little peace and quiet." He glanced at her. She was leaning against the tree all right, but she was almost as rigid as a soldier standing at attention. "Did you forget how to relax?"

"No." Yet she knew that relaxing was a major effort for her lately. "Maybe," she conceded. She followed up her admission with a rueful grin. "There's not much opportunity to unwind back home."

He grinned and shook his head.

It seemed to be a private joke and she wanted in on it. She prodded his ribs with her elbow. "What?"

What a fool he'd been to go away and leave her in someone else's care. He'd been asking for it, he thought with the hindsight of experience. But all that was behind him. The future loomed before him; holding out promises he meant to collect on.

"Funny, whenever I pictured you saying 'back home,' I assumed you'd mean here."

Carole Anne frowned. She didn't want to get into that. "This isn't home anymore."

He hoped she didn't say that to her aunt. He didn't want to see the woman upset. "Aunt Connie would be hurt to hear you say that."

Carole Anne shifted uncomfortably. She knew he was right. But the truth was the truth. This *wasn't* home anymore. Not really. Restless, she recast her line. The hook snagged in the tree overhead. Terrific. "Aunt Connie doesn't understand."

Setting his own pole aside, Jeff rose and untangled her hook for her. "Not all of us do. What's the attraction out there?"

She waited until he'd sat down again before casting out. She did it with a snap of her wrist. The line sang like a tiny mosquito before it hit the water. "Life."

It was a standard, evasive answer. He'd thought she could do better. Maybe she didn't have an answer anymore, he speculated. That was hopeful.

"I haven't exactly been treating dead people in Belle's Grove, Carole Anne."

She realized that it was like trying to describe colors to a man who couldn't see. "It's hard to explain if you've never wanted it."

No, he'd never wanted it. The only thing he'd ever wanted was to be useful. And to have her. "And now you have it," he said mildly, as if he was reciting tomorrow's forecast.

She stared intently at the lake. "Yes, I do."

The line in her jaw was growing rigid. He wondered if she knew. "Are you happy?"

She glared at him. Wasn't he ever going to stop this meandering inquisition? "Yes, I'm happy!"

His grin disarmed the fuse that was about to blow. "You're scaring the fish."

She shrugged ruefully, annoyed that she had lost control for a moment. She mentally counted to ten, then continued. "This town might be very nice for a picture postcard at Christmastime—" she gestured around with her free hand "—but it wasn't enough for me."

He caught the slip and was on it with the tenacity of Sherlock Holmes working to unravel a mysterious clue. "'Wasn't'?"

She realized her mistake as soon as the word was out of her mouth. "I mean, isn't." She knew what he was thinking. It was the same thing that her aunt was hoping for. Carole Anne couldn't deal with that. "Jeff, I'm not coming back here to live."

He shrugged as if indifferent, then lazily cast out his line. It hit the water not too far away from hers. "No one said you should. If I'm digging, it's because I'm just trying to understand things in my own, plodding, country-doctor sort of way."

Next he was going to kick the dirt and say, "Aw, shucks." That kind of behavior might have been expected of the old Jefferson Drumm, but she had glimpsed another man in place of the boy she had once known. He might be modest, but not disparagingly so.

"Ha! You were never 'plodding.'"

He slanted her a reproving look. "You seemed to think so." Otherwise, why would she have left?

She had that coming, but she definitely didn't want to go into it again with him. And she definitely didn't want him to know that there had been nights, when she was alone, that she would lie awake going over her life inch by inch, wondering what it would have been like if she had married him instead of Cal. What it would have been like if she *had* bought into forever.

But all that was behind her. She had been bruised enough to last a lifetime and she wasn't up to any more romantic adventures, not even with Jeff. Perhaps most especially not with Jeff.

But there was something she had to know. "Why didn't you ever leave here? After you graduated medical school, you could have gone to any major city and built up an impressive practice."

"I have a practice," he pointed out. It wasn't in a huge multi-storied building, but it suited him.

He was being purposely perverse. "You could have been wealthy."

He looked at her for a long moment before answering. "I am."

She drew her brows together. He was driving a beat-up old pickup with a broken taillight. And Aunt Connie said he was still living in the house where he had grown up. "You are?"

Her skepticism was so pronounced, he wondered what had happened to the girl he had once known. She would have understood without his having to explain.

"Do you know that in some cultures, a man's wealth is measured by the number of horses he owns? In others, it's the number of eagle feathers in his headdress that earned him respect." He looked at her significantly. "Still others, it's the number of people he could call friend."

She dug in stubbornly. He could have made something of himself, done research, amounted to something. Instead he had chosen to remain in a backwater town that would never fully appreciate him. Because she cared about him, it bothered her. "Couldn't you have called people 'friend' and still made money?"

He wondered if she was being mercenary, or just arguing a point. He hadn't noticed anything flashy about her when she arrived. He decided that this was all academic, but he had to hear it from her. "Is money that important to you, Carole Anne?"

She squared her shoulders, defensive again. "No, but not being poor is. Being able to give Brandon anything he wants is."

He stroked his chin elaborately, like a simpleminded man trying to come to terms with new information. "Now I'm not all that up on new trends in child rearing—living in the sticks and all—but I always thought that if you gave your child a lot of love, everything else would somehow work itself out."

Was he trying to accuse her of substituting possessions for attention? "Brandon has love."

He'd guessed as much, seeing them together last night and this morning. If anything, she was too protective of the boy. "So what you're saying, in essence, is that he doesn't need toys with a fancy price tag on them?"

She blinked, confused for a moment. "You're twisting things."

"Not me." He shrugged elaborately, playing the rube. "I'm a simple country doctor, remember?"

She almost laughed out loud. He'd gotten devious since she last knew him. "You're no more simple than Albert Schweitzer was."

He pretended to think over her comment. "As I recall, he wasn't much on big cities, either."

Carole Anne let out a long sigh. "All right, got a handkerchief?"

He set down his pole and fished it out of his back pocket. "Why? Have I moved you to tears?"

"No." She opened the handkerchief and then waved it overhead. "I surrender." Carole Anne shoved the handkerchief back into his hand.

Intrigued, he repocketed it. Jeff didn't bother picking up his pole again. The line bobbed up and down in the water, untouched. "To what?"

"To the rhetoric." She was no match for his stubbornness today.

"I've got a better idea."

She heard a smile in his voice and looked at him, suddenly wary. "Oh? Like what?"

Slowly, Jeff took the fishing pole out of her hands and placed it on the ground. His eyes darkened ever so slightly as he took her into his arms. "Like me surrendering to something I've been wanting to do for eight long years."

She stiffened, but couldn't force herself to pull away. "Jeff, this isn't a good idea."

God, he wanted her. It had been something he had been denying all this time. He thought he'd successfully buried his desire for her. Sitting here next to her, with the warm sun bathing them both, he realized he'd been lying to himself. He had never gotten over her.

"It's not an idea. It's a reality."

Before she could utter another protest or recapture the senses that had suddenly fled, Jeff kissed her. Kissed her and made the years between then and now completely disappear.

Except that Jeff had never kissed her this way before. Never disarmed her soul and made her feel lost and disoriented, as if she was a lone towel in a washing machine set on spin cycle. Before, Jeff's kisses had been sweet and boyishly tender. They had made her sigh.

There was nothing about the boy to be found here. And the man took her breath away as well as the very ground beneath her.

The chemistry she had detected when she first saw him standing in Aunt Connie's living room yesterday exploded, spontaneously combusting the test tube and scorching everything in its path like lava consuming the ground.

Oh, God.

Carole Anne closed her eyes and momentarily let herself be swept away by needs, by hunger, by the desire for well-being. Feelings she had, she thought, so cleverly hidden away. Everything dissolved in the heat of his mouth as it met hers over and over again. Like a lone survivor attempting to paddle a canoe through the white water rapids, she navigated wildly, just trying to stay afloat, just trying to hold on to a shred of her senses.

It wasn't easy.

As he feasted on her mouth, Jeff opened up floodgates within her. The waters came rushing out to meet him. She clung to him, her mouth hungry for his, hungry for what he had to give her.

She was everything he remembered and more. So much more. When they had last kissed, they had been children with the dew of innocence about them. They weren't children any longer. Separately, they had traveled down rocky paths that had demanded a great deal from them, and they had managed to survive it all. The passions they had acquired and required emerged.

This was adult, mature, and devastatingly mindless.

Jeff forced himself to back away. He knew that if they went too fast, the road would burn up beneath their feet.

And then the final destination could not be reached. He very much wanted to get there.

He leaned his forehead against hers and waited for several beats of his erratic heart before he sufficiently caught his breath. He grinned to himself, completely unembarrassed by the fact that she had left him breathless. "Welcome back."

It took her longer to catch her breath. This was insane.

She pulled away, though everything inside her begged to remain in the shelter of his arms. But there was no such thing as shelter and she wasn't about to fall into that trap. She wasn't going to believe that there was. "Don't get the wrong idea."

He cupped her chin before she could scramble to her feet. "Lady, I have lots of ideas."

And she wasn't going to like any of them. She couldn't let herself be weak. What she needed most was a friend, not a lover. Lovers left. Friends hung on. "I want us to be friends."

Jeff nodded slowly. "That's part of it."

She had to put a stop to it here. "That's all of it. Thomas Hardy's right. You can't go home again." And she couldn't return to the safe feeling she had once known. Or to the belief that love conquered all. It didn't conquer, it vanquished its victims and then faded away like summer roses.

He wasn't about to let her hide behind trite philosophies. "Thomas Hardy is dead. He was a soured old man who never understood the power of optimism and faith. He has nothing to do with you and me."

Panic began to claw at her. She wasn't going to buy into the dream. She wasn't. Dreams never came true, at least, not romantic ones. She had made her life and was going to stick with it. "There is no you and me."

He wasn't going to let her lie to him or to herself. "Carole Anne, there has *always* been a you and me. The definition has just evolved with time, that's all." From friends to a great deal more.

"Well, the definition of who and what we are now is that you're a doctor in Belle's Grove and I'm a free-lance writer, emphasis on 'free,'" she said stubbornly.

Jeff pretended to solemnly raise his hand, taking an oath. "It was never my intention to try to clip your wings, Carole Anne."

"Yeah, right." Because of their past, of what they had shared, she was able to eye him with amusement. For the moment, the truth behind his words was pushed aside. "Do you remember when we used to come to this lake?"

Vividly. More than that, he remembered coming here the day he learned that she had eloped. He'd driven the three hundred miles from college like a man possessed, tearing down the back roads in record time until he reached the lake. Somehow, he had hoped—prayed—that she'd be here, waiting for him. That it was all some horrible misunderstanding.

It was only when he'd arrived and found the lake desolate that he knew what his mother had told him over the telephone was true. Carole Anne was gone. Gone without so much as a word. Gone with his best friend.

But there was no point in saying any of this to her now. Instead he kept his voice calm. "Yes. Those were long, lazy summer days." He glanced at her. "Not unlike this one. We used to go skinny-dipping."

Carole Anne couldn't help laughing as she remembered. "Your mother would have taken a strap to you if she had known."

He grinned, enjoying the sound of her laughter. At least that hadn't changed. "I don't think she would have been all that delighted with you, either."

She placed a hand delicately to her breast. "I was an innocent ten, led astray by an older man."

She made him sound ancient. "Twelve wasn't that old," he protested.

AUNT CONNIE'S WEDDING 69

That wasn't the way she remembered it. "You were always old, Jeff." She smiled fondly at him. "You always had the weight of the world on your shoulders." She studied him now. "You seem less somber now than you did then." It was as if the years had gone in reverse for him.

Jeff shrugged. "I guess I realized that I couldn't do it all. I suppose back then I was just trying to make it up to my mother that my dad was gone."

Carole Anne laid a hand over his. "I'm sorry about your mother."

He nodded. Death was part of life. It was something he had come to terms with on a professional level. Personally, it had been much more difficult for him. His mother was the first patient he had ever lost.

"Yeah, so am I. I'd like to think they're together now." He shrugged off the somber mood and nodded toward the lake. "You want to take a dip for old times' sake?"

She glanced down at her halter and white shorts. "I don't have a suit."

He grinned, a hint of mischief glinting his eyes. "No, I meant, like we used to."

She looked at him, stunned. She hadn't expected this from Dr. Drumm. But the kiss should have warned her. "Nude?"

He could have sworn embarrassment tinged her cheeks. He found it endearing. And arousing. "I'm a doctor, remember? You haven't got a thing I haven't seen before."

"Right, but you haven't seen it on me." She held up her hands just in case he had any ideas. "Not in eighteen years, at any rate."

He nodded, picking up his pole. It had only been a fleeting thought. "Your loss. It's hot."

She looked at him knowingly. "And if we go skinny-dipping, it'll get a lot hotter."

Exactly what he was hoping for. Jeff grinned. "Nice to hear, Carole Anne. Nice to hear." His pole was jiggling, but he seemed oblivious to it.

Carole Anne reached over to grab his fishing pole before it was pulled out of his hand. "I think you've got a bite on your line."

He grasped the pole, wrapping his hands around it. His eyes never left hers.

"I sincerely hope so."

Carole Anne decided that it was more prudent not to argue about this, too. As it was, she had let her mind run riot with Jeff's suggestion. It *was* a hot day. And Jeff had filled out a great deal since he was twelve.

"I could use some help here."

She knew he didn't need it. But she sidled up to him and wrapped her hands over his.

For a moment, it was just like old times.

If she didn't think about the kiss.

And she tried not to. Very, very hard.

Chapter Five

There were three cookbooks spread out over the blue Formica countertop, all turned to pages showing photographs of wedding cakes. Connie frowned as she glanced from one to another while fussing over a breakfast that Carole Anne wasn't in the mood to eat.

Connie wouldn't have been glancing at any wedding cakes at all, except that Carole Anne had insisted that she make a decision as to the kind of cake she wanted at the reception. The wedding was less than two weeks away now. Carole Anne had been appalled to discover that no real arrangements had actually been made yet.

Figuratively rolling up her sleeves, her niece had informed her that there was no more time to waste. Connie was of the opinion that things always had a way of taking care of themselves and events always dovetailed to work out.

Carole Anne didn't subscribe to the same philosophy that her aunt did. She was attempting her best to make Aunt Connie aware of reality.

With a patient sigh, she pushed a book forward just as Connie flipped the last pancake on the griddle. "Maybe we could go with this one—"

"Well, look who's up and about." Connie fairly beamed as she tilted her head to look around Carole Anne's shoulder toward the back staircase.

Carole Anne turned to see her son fairly bounce into the room. He looked completely different from the little boy who had been lying in bed yesterday. Relief fanned through her. "Well, that was quick."

"It's the country air," Brandon informed her with the attitude of one who knew these kinds of things.

Carole Anne crossed her arms at her chest, amused. "Oh, it is, is it?" She looked over Brandon's head at her aunt. "And who told you that?" As if she didn't already know.

"Dr. Jeff." Brandon negotiated his way onto the stool, climbing up on his knees first. "He said I'd be up and around in no time 'cause it was so clean around here. And he was right." Brandon's bottom met the seat and he stuck his short legs out in front of him. They dangled six inches shy of the floor. "Do I get to go fishing today?"

Dr. Jeff. That would have been her second guess. She didn't need him brainwashing Brandon with this kind of nonsense.

"I'm surrounded by conspirators," Carole Anne murmured under her breath.

Aunt Connie moved the cookbooks aside carefully and leaned across the counter to look Brandon over to her own satisfaction. The boy looked fully recovered to her. "No, just people who love you," Connie assured her. She moved a place mat in front of Brandon on the countertop and laid a fork and napkin on the side. "Pancakes stacked high?"

The dark, fine hair shimmied as Brandon bobbed his head up and down. "Sure!" He grasped his fork in his hand, ready. "But what about fishing?" he pressed his mother again.

She hated disappointing him, but she doubted that it would be possible, no matter what Jeff had said yesterday. It was Monday and she had no doubts that Jeff was busy. She brushed a hand over Brandon's head. "Honey, I think you're going to have to postpone it, I really don't think that Dr. Jeff'll be available—"

"Until later this afternoon."

Carole Anne swung around just as Jeff walked in through the back door. He laid his hands on her shoulders by way of a greeting, but he was looking at Brandon. "Hi, Brandon. Feeling okay?"

Brandon's face split into a smile that threatened to make his eyes disappear. "I'm feeling just great, thank you."

"Polite, too," Jeff murmured to Carole Anne, his words brushing up against her ear.

She had to brace her shoulders to keep the shiver from materializing.

Jeff picked up a piece of toast from the plate that Connie had placed before him. "I like to hear that from all my patients." Taking a bite of the toast, he ruffled Brandon's hair with his other hand.

Brandon looked pleased at the attention. Carole Anne worried about his becoming attached to Jeff and being disappointed. After all, they were only going to be here two weeks. She moved to the boy's other side.

Brandon felt like the best part of a sandwich, with his mother on one side and Dr. Jeff on the other.

"Do you just walk in here any time you want?" Carole Anne asked Jeff.

She reminded him of a lioness guarding her cub. He wouldn't have thought that of her. It made him smile. "No, usually just for morning coffee." He dropped down onto the stool next to Brandon's. Connie handed him a mug of steaming black coffee. "Thanks, Aunt Connie."

The scene rankled Carole Anne. She felt as if he was crowding in on her unfairly. "She's not your Aunt Connie, she's my Aunt Connie."

He swallowed the sip of coffee in his mouth. His eyes were crystal green, and knowing. "Ah, getting territorial, are we?"

"Now, now, children," Aunt Connie chided in the same voice she had used with Carole Anne when she'd misbehaved as a child. "There's certainly enough of me to go around."

The sound of bubbles being blown in a glass interfered with Carole Anne's silent self-reproach for acting so petty and childish. Brandon was dissolving in a fit of giggles in his glass of milk.

Carole Anne took the glass from Brandon before he drowned in it. A small smile lifted her lips. "And what's so funny?"

Brandon looked up at his mother with a milky mustache and goatee. "Aunt Connie called you and Dr. Jeff children."

Beating her to the napkin on the place mat, Jeff took it and, rather than wipe off Brandon's dairy disguise, handed the napkin to the boy. "It's all in the perspective, Brandon. So, how's two o'clock sound?"

Brandon solemnly wiped his face then handed the napkin back to Jeff. "Did they finish cleaning the lake already?"

A smile tugged at Jeff's lips, but he remained straight-faced. "It's spanking clean." He glanced at Carole Anne. She was wearing a cotton T-shirt that clung just enough to her breasts to make his mouth dry. He took another sip of coffee, but it didn't help. "Your mom and I checked it out yesterday for you."

Connie debated making another batch of pancakes, but knew from experience that all Jeff ever took in the morning when he worked was toast and coffee. Ah, well, at least Brandon was eating.

"You unsettled her, Jefferson." Connie leaned forward, lowering her voice as if that would keep Carole Anne from hearing. "She hardly slept at all last night. Again," she added significantly.

Carole Anne didn't appreciate being the topic of discussion, especially when she was standing right there. She looked at her aunt accusingly. "How would you know?"

Connie placed the pan in the sink and turned on the faucet. "My room's next to yours, dear," Connie reminded her. "You spun around like a top all night." Connie raised her voice to be heard above the water. "The springs on your bed creak."

Carole Anne sighed. There weren't going to be any secrets until she went back to L.A. "I've got a lot on my mind."

Jeff had drained his cup and set it down on the counter. Getting off the stool, he slipped an arm around Carole Anne's shoulders and gave her a quick squeeze that surprised her. "Only good thoughts, I hope."

She eased away, staring at him. "You certainly have changed."

A lot had happened in eight years. A lot to shape his life. He was responsible for people's lives, had a seat on the town council, and headed up a very badly needed volunteer fire department. The shy, awkward boy had gotten lost in the shuffle and mercifully disappeared to make room for the man.

He grinned. "So've you." He nodded to where she was standing. "You weren't this skittish before."

She crossed her arms in front of her chest, as stoic-looking as a cigar-store Indian. "I've grown up."

Jeff smiled, thinking of yesterday, of the way she had felt in his arms. Of the kiss that had burned its way into his dreams last night. Yes, she had grown up. They both had "I know."

She could tell exactly what Jeff was thinking by the way his eyes slid over her. "Don't you have a clinic to see to?"

He thought of his appointment book, the one Alice oversaw like a zealous pit bull. "It'll be a light day today, I hope. But I should get going." He looked over his shoulder at Brandon. The boy immediately brightened at the attention sent his way. "Have your mom bring you by the clinic at two."

"I'll need to get a pole," Brandon began hesitantly, looking at his mother.

"Already packed," Jeff assured him. "I put them in the back of my truck this morning just in case."

Brandon's eyes were as large as the wooden coasters Aunt Connie kept stacked on the living-room coffee table. "Really?"

Jeff did his best to look solemn as he crossed his heart. "Doctors never lie."

Carole Anne cleared her throat as she eyed Jeff. Any deeper and he'd need a shovel.

Jeff looked unfazed by her censure. "In small towns, at any rate," he added. "See you later, Brandon." He turned, looking over Brandon's head at Carole Anne as he made his way to the back door. "You, too. Thanks for the coffee, Aunt Connie." He winked at the older woman, who flushed with obvious pleasure.

Only when the back door closed did Carole Anne relax enough to sit down at the breakfast bar. She picked up her mug from the counter. It was ice cold. She didn't notice. Her mind was on Jeff and on the way he seemed to upend her each time she saw him.

"Does he really barge in like that every morning?"

Connie made a clucking sound at Carole Anne's choice of words. "Jefferson didn't barge in, Carole Anne. I invited him."

Carole Anne arched a brow as she looked at her aunt's innocent expression. "When?"

Connie stopped clearing away dishes to consider Carole Anne's question. She smiled, delighted when the answer came to her. "Four years ago." The smile faded slightly as she added, "When Mitzi passed on."

"And he's been coming over in the morning ever since?" Carole Anne asked incredulously.

Connie had no idea what the fuss was about. Clearly Carole Anne had forgotten what it meant to be neighborly. Living out in Los Angeles couldn't be good for her, Connie decided, no matter what her niece said to the contrary. It was apparent to Connie that Carole Anne had lost more than a little of her innocent faith residing among the glittery people.

Taking the frying pan out of the sink, she shook it free of water and began to dry it. "His mother was my best friend. Since she passed away, I guess I've kind of taken to mothering him." In that sense, they had helped each other, she thought, each filling the gap that Mitzi Drumm had left in their lives.

Carole Anne stared at her aunt. "Mothering him? Aunt Connie, he's thirty years old."

Connie deliberately set down the frying pan on the counter and looked at Carole Anne for a long moment, searching for the little girl she had once known. She was in there somewhere, Connie was certain. It was just going to take time to get her out.

"No one's ever too old for a mother." Connie glanced over toward Brandon. The boy was polishing off the last of his breakfast, "Remember that, Brandon."

"Yes, ma'am," he answered respectfully, his mouth full of pancakes. Syrup dribbled down the center of his chin in the wake of his words.

Connie resumed tidying up. "Anyway, Jefferson stops by for coffee and a little conversation on his way to the clinic every morning. His visits brighten up my day. Of course—" Connie placed the pan in the cupboard, then turned to eye Carole Anne shrewdly "—if he was married, I suppose he'd stop coming by."

Carole Anne took the next-to-last piece of pancake from Brandon's plate and popped it into her mouth. "Maybe his wife won't know how to make coffee."

Connie took the empty plate away. "You make excellent coffee, dear."

Carole Anne had had enough matchmaking for one day. "Aunt Connie." There was a warning note in Carole Anne's voice.

With the tactically shrewd instincts of a Napoleon, Connie moved one of the cookbooks back to the center of the counter. "About this cake, dear." Connie tapped the glossy page. "Do you think it should be three tiers or four?"

Brandon rose to his knees on the stool and peered down at the photograph. "Four," he said decisively. It meant more to eat. "And it should be chocolate frosting, not 'nilla."

"*V*anilla," Carole Anne corrected. "And all wedding cakes have vanilla frosting." She caught herself as she realized that she had been listening to the sound of the engine as Jeff's truck pulled away. It was gone now.

Connie bit the inside of her cheek, thinking. "There's no written law about it." Her brown eyes met Brandon's as she considered the matter carefully, like a bullfighter attempting to decide which way to best approach a bull. "And Emmett *does* like chocolate more than vanilla." She studied the photograph and frowned. "Vanilla is such a bland flavor, really. No color, no sparkle." Connie closed the book and nodded her head, decision made. "Chocolate it is."

Carole Anne sighed. She rose from the stool and crossed to the coffeepot on the stove. Resigned, she poured herself another cup, black as usual. She had a feeling she was going to need it.

* * *

At two o'clock, Carole Anne pulled onto the asphalt driveway that led up to the Belle's Grove Medical Clinic like a fading royal black carpet. Brandon was out of the car before she had a chance to close her own door.

She stopped and looked at the clinic for a moment. The exterior of the building had hardly changed from the days when Aunt Connie would bring her here to be treated for a host of childhood ailments. There had been no add-ons, no expansion. It was still a one-story building that looked more like someone's home than a place where medicine and kindness were dispensed.

In his time, Doc Williams had been the embodiment of a country doctor to her, handing out lollipops and antibiotics along with sage advise whenever it was called for. A perennial bachelor married to his work, he had been there for her to gently unravel the terrifying mysteries of womanhood when she was twelve and her body began going through changes. He had made everything seem so natural, so right.

In the autumn of his years, he had taken an interest in Jeff after Jeff had done some work on his roof. With no family of his own except for a sister in Detroit, Doc Williams took Jeff under his wing and insisted on paying for his medical school expenses. He had said hands as skilled as Jeff's shouldn't be wasted. Jeff had stopped turning down his offer after that.

She half expected to see Doc Williams standing on the porch now, nursing an old hickory pipe, the smoke curling above his head in a wispy halo.

But there was a potted benjamina on the porch where he had once stood. Times changed. She knew that better than anyone.

Carole Anne took Brandon's hand and climbed up the stairs. She noted absently that the rickety third step had finally been repaired. She smiled fondly, remembering. Doc Williams had always meant to get to that.

Close up, she realized that the building, rather than being the weather-beaten, aging structure it had once been, was sporting a new coat of paint. And cracked shingles had been replaced. Someone had lovingly restored it to its former dignity.

She remembered that carpentry had always been a hobby for Jeff. To help out his mother financially, he had picked up odd jobs building things for people while he was still attending high school. Carole Anne ran her hand along the refinished handrail. Obviously it had turned into a skill.

She was just admiring the finely carved front door when it flew open.

A woman with short-cropped, bright red hair was herding a gaggle of small children before her. She all but plowed into Carole Anne and Brandon. Carole Anne yanked Brandon to the side to give the woman room a second before recognition set in.

Janice Harper was a little more maturely figured than she had been eight years ago, but there was no mistaking the lightning-fast grin.

"Carole Anne!" she squealed, and four little faces turned to look at the woman their mother was greeting. Janice released the younger two to grasp Carole Anne's hands in hers. "I heard you were back." Sharp green eyes that missed nothing made short work of scrutinizing Carole Anne from head to foot. "Sorry I had to miss your welcome home party, the twins were sick. You look terrific. As a matter of fact, so terrific I shouldn't even be speaking to you." She looked at Brandon and gave him an abbreviated appraisal. "Is this precious child yours?"

Janice had always had a habit of barreling through life at ninety miles an hour. Her main difficulty was remembering to apply the brakes. The collection of children around her testified to that.

Carole Anne placed a protective hand on Brandon's shoulder. "This is my son, Brandon."

Janice eyed Carole Anne's slender figure. "Just the one," she concluded, sighing wistfully. Carole Anne nodded, confirming her statement. Janice gestured to her brood. "I've got five."

Carole Anne raised a brow. She saw only four.

"Julius is in school, thank God," Janice rattled on. "The rest of these are heading that way, but not soon enough for me." She laughed good-naturedly, but there was a note of weariness in her voice. "I never fully appreciated what my mother went through until now."

One of the little girls grabbed onto Janice's skirt and began tugging her in the direction of the parking lot. "Ice cream, Mommy. You said."

Janice let herself be dragged off. "Well, stop by the house when you get a chance." She was halfway to the car and digging through a cavernous purse for keys when she looked up. "Oh, almost forgot, it's Janice Winters now. Finally caught Brett."

She grinned like a hunter talking about having bagged an elusive prey. Then she looked down at the crowd pooling about her legs. It was obvious to Carole Anne that Janice loved the children and just as obvious that she needed a small vacation. Or perhaps a large one.

Janice unlocked the car door and the children scampered inside the minivan. "Sometimes I wonder who caught who." She snapped two seatbelts in place. "Gotta fly. Call me!" she threw over her shoulder just before she disappeared into the violet-colored vehicle.

Brandon looked up at his mother. "She sure talks fast."

Carole Anne nodded with a smile. "She always did." She turned toward the oak door and grasped the brass handle. "Well, let's go in."

A wave of nostalgia washed over Carole Anne as soon as she walked inside the clinic. He'd kept the wooden floors, she noticed, looking down at her feet.

Freshly polished, sparkling clean, two sides lined with dark blue sofas that had pale yellow flowers sprinkled across the cushions, the sight of the front room catapulted Carole Anne back over a span of almost twenty years. She was standing in the doorway, clutching her aunt's hand while the woman murmured soothingly that the booster shot Doc Williams was going to give her wasn't really going to hurt.

Carole Anne blinked, returning to the present.

There was a large, knotty pine desk placed near the back of the waiting room. That was new. A formidable-looking nurse with iron-gray hair stood guarding the appointment book. Her expression reminded Carole Anne of a protective German shepherd. The woman was very blatantly sizing Carole Anne up.

"Can I help you?"

Carole Anne felt as if she was back in elementary school, forced to recite a poem she couldn't remember. "I'd like to see Jeff—the doctor," Carole Anne corrected herself quickly.

The woman peered at her over the top of her half glasses. "Do you have an appointment?"

The only way to beard this lioness was to bluff. "Yes."

The nurse pressed one short-nailed finger against the book. "Name?"

So much for bluffing, although she *did* have an appointment of sorts. Or, at least, Brandon did. "Carole Anne Wellsley, but—"

The nurse scanned the appointment book with the efficiency of one who had been doing this a long time. She raised her eyes and looked at Carole Anne accusingly. "You're not listed."

Brandon had no idea what was going on, but he knew he was supposed to be here. He gripped the edge of the desk and stood on his toes to get a better look at the woman who was guarding this doctor. "Dr. Jeff's supposed to take me fishing."

The nurse leaned over the desk, her expression softening an iota. "Dr. Jeff is in surgery."

Carole Anne looked around at the wood-framed structure. Like most of the buildings in Belle's Grove, the medical clinic had been standing for well over a hundred years. The last she remembered, there were no facilities to conduct an operation. The nurse probably meant that Jeff was setting a fracture.

"In here?" Carole Anne raised a brow skeptically.

The nurse was already dismissing her as she looked down at her appointment book and began writing. "Man's appendix bursts, it doesn't take note of the location."

If he was performing an emergency appendectomy, he certainly couldn't take a small boy fishing. Carole Anne looked down at Brandon and offered the boy a comforting smile. "I guess you're going to have to take a rain check, honey."

Wispy brows drew together in a dark line. "I can go fishing in the rain?"

Carole Anne laughed. "No, I mean—"

She stopped as she saw Jeff emerging out of a room that could have doubled as a parlor. She remembered Doc Williams examining her in that room. Jeff looked tired, but obviously very satisfied with himself. He was dressed in a green surgical gown, as was the woman walking next to him. A very pretty woman.

Carole Anne tensed and told herself that she had no idea why.

"You look funny," Brandon told Jeff as he hurried over to him.

Jeff looked up, startled. He had been deeply involved in discussing Joe Walsh's prognosis with Sheila. The sound of a young voice piping into the midst of his thoughts disoriented Jeff for a moment. It had turned out to be a long day, full of sneezes, earaches and rashes. And then Joe had come in, complaining of a sharp pain in his gut a minute before he had keeled over.

"Oh, Brandon. Hello." Jeff rubbed the bridge of his nose. The surgical mask had been on too tight, but there had be no time to think of his own comfort. Joe's appendix had ruptured right there in his office. "Is it two o'clock already?"

Carole Anne crossed to her son and laid a hand on his small shoulders. "Yes, but your nurse said you were in surgery so we'll just—" She began to usher Brandon toward the door.

Jeff caught her arm. He had to be fast. Carole Anne was getting positively slippery. "Don't be in such a hurry to 'just'." Releasing his hold on her arm, he winked at her and she reacted with a completely adolescent fluttery feeling in the pit of her stomach.

He looked down at Brandon. "I can be ready in about ten minutes, if that's okay with you?"

Brandon lifted his shoulders and let them drop. "Sure. I'm not going anywhere."

Carole Anne glanced at her watch. She had an appointment in half an hour with Martha Cooper, the best pastry maker in Belle's Grove, to discuss baking Aunt Connie's wedding cake. She supposed she could stay here with Brandon until Jeff was ready.

Jeff turned to the woman at his side. "Sheila, the ambulance transport for Joe should be here in about fifteen minutes or so. Fill them in, will you? And hold down the fort."

Sheila, a statuesque brunette with a dimple in her right cheek that Carole Anne hated instantly, smiled. "Will do. Going fishing?"

Jeff exchanged a conspiratorial look with Brandon. "Yep."

The woman's smile widened and looked far too sexy to Carole Anne. "Have fun, doctor. You've certainly earned it."

"Thanks. Oh, one more thing," he called after her. She stopped and turned, waiting. "Would you also mind calling Joe's family? They're going to be wondering why he didn't come home after his office visit."

"Sure thing." Sheila hurried to the consultation room. Except that she made it look as if she was moving in slow motion. Slow, sultry slow motion.

"Who's that?" Carole Anne laced her hands together in front of her as she looked at Jeff innocently.

The performance couldn't have fooled a ten-year-old, Jeff thought, pleased with himself. If she was jealous, it meant she cared. And he could certainly work with that.

"That's Sheila Granger, my nurse practitioner." He moved toward the desk as he shed his gown. He was wearing jeans and a T-shirt that adhered to finely shaped pectorals underneath. "And this is Alice Henderson," he gestured toward the woman who had given Carole Anne the once-over. "The rock upon which my office is built."

"We've met." Alice hardly cracked a smile. "The rest of your afternoon's free, so I guess you can go...fishing." She gave Carole Anne one last penetrating look and went to look in on the patient's condition.

Carole Anne felt like a parolee in the presence of a former warden. "How long does she go on giving a person the third degree?"

He laughed. A tough-as-nails nurse who was also a grandmother three times over, Alice was very protective of him in her own crusty way. "Until she decides whether or not she likes them."

Carole Anne looked toward the room where Alice had disappeared. "Well, the jury obviously appears to be out about me."

Not as far as I'm concerned. "Don't worry, you'll win her over."

She'd almost walked right into that one. "I'm not worried and I'm not going to be around long enough to win anyone over." She softened immediately as she looked at him. Jeff *did* look a little frayed around the edges. "Are you sure you're not too tired to go?"

Brandon whimpered a protest but she just squeezed his hand. She didn't want Jeff falling face-forward into the lake just to keep a promise to her son.

But Jeff shook his head adamantly. "A little fishing sounds like heaven to me right now." He slung his surgical livery over his arm. "Hang on, partner," he told Brandon. "Just let me get into something that doesn't have the color green in it."

With that, he walked to the back, whistling an old song. Belatedly, Carole Anne realized that it was the one he had considered to be "their" song. She frowned, but to her surprise, her heart wasn't in it.

Chapter Six

Jeff was as good as his word. It took him just under the time limit he had given Brandon to change. He emerged from his office, his shirttails trailing behind him as he moved quickly. She noticed that his hair was just the slightest bit mussed and he was tucking his shirt into the waistband of his faded blue jeans.

It took her back.

All the way to when they were both attending high school. Jeff would come hurrying across her front lawn, a bulging backpack hanging from his arm as he struggled to pull himself together. But he was never late. He was always there to walk with her to the school bus stop.

She didn't realize that she was smiling.

Jeff crossed to the far end of the waiting room where she sat, a magazine held open on her lap. It was upside down. She hadn't even bothered to glance at it. He grinned as he took it from her and closed it, then dropped it on the long oak table.

"You look nice that way." Her brows rose quizzically. "Smiling," Jeff explained.

Brandon jumped up, hitting the side of the table. He sent three magazines tumbling to the floor, then scooped them up quickly, hoping he hadn't made Dr. Jeff angry.

Carole Anne ran her tongue over her lower lip unconsciously. She saw something flash in Jeff's eyes just a moment before he shut it away. Desire? Why did that create such a rush within her? She didn't want him feeling that way about her.

"I wasn't aware that I was," she said self-consciously. "Smiling," she added.

"Those are the best kinds of smiles." He leaned over and kissed her quickly. Just a fleeting, friendly kiss. His lips barely came in contact with hers. Yet the act spoke volumes. Volumes she was certain that she didn't want propped open.

For if they were opened, the consequences would be too great. Give your heart, get it back as confetti. She'd learned that the hard way. Well, she wasn't a fool. It only took once to teach her.

Besides, Jeff was married to Belle's Grove and she had outgrown Belle's Grove a long time ago. They had no future, only a past.

She had so many sound arguments why she shouldn't feel anything, why she *couldn't* feel anything, and yet here she was, feeling. That one tiny kiss had touched off so many things in so many ways, like a pebble dropped in a pond, forming rings. It warmed her, made her feel special, safe. Made her—

A complete idiot, she thought.

Carole Anne shifted away from Jeff as if she had just touched fire with her bare hand. Alice had returned to her post and was scrutinizing her again like a sergeant waiting for a miscreant private to jump KP and go AWOL.

AUNT CONNIE'S WEDDING 89

Carole Anne cleared her throat, hating the fact that she felt so unsettled. This was Jeff, for God's sake, Jeff, who she had grown up with.

Jeff, a small voice within her whispered, who she had run out on.

"Well, if you're going fishing, you two better get started," she mumbled. Wanting to get away until she could compose herself, she crossed to the door. "I have an appointment to see about ordering Aunt Connie's wedding cake." She looked to Jeff for support. "She wants chocolate."

Jeff nodded as he joined her. Brandon hurried after them. "Great choice."

When did his grin get so terribly sexy? "You're no help," she complained.

As she reached for the doorknob, the door opened. Melody Beauchamp, wearing a white sundress that belonged on a body one size smaller, blocked her exit.

The woman reeked of sensuality, Giorgio perfume and determination. Melody and she had never moved in the same circles in high school and the greeting Carole Anne was about to utter died on her lips. Melody moved past her as if she wasn't even in the room.

As if following the beep of a homing device, Melody headed straight for Jeff. She left approximately six inches between them. None when she inhaled deeply, Carole Anne noted. Melody brushed her well-manicured hand with its bright red nails dramatically against her chest.

"Oh, Jeff."

Melody uttered his name so breathlessly, she would have gotten first prize in a Marilyn Monroe impersonator contest, Carole Anne thought, only slightly amused.

"I'm so sorry to barge in like this, but I just can't seem to get rid of this nagging cough." Melody blinked, her long lashes sweeping her high cheekbones delicately, like twin butterflies coming in for a landing. "You remember my cough, don't you?"

There was no way he could *not* remember. She had demonstrated it rather blatantly in his office. Jeff attempted his best to be diplomatic. "I'm just on my way out, Melody."

"It would only take you a minute." The woman eyed the consultation room like a cat watching a sparrow flutter by her window and yearning for a chance to spring at it.

For a moment Carole Anne thought that Jeff was going to tell them to wait while he looked into Melody's so-called cough center, but then he surprised her by crossing to the reception desk.

"Tell Sheila that she's got a patient," he instructed Alice. Turning to Melody, he squeezed her arm reassuringly. "Sheila will see to all your needs."

"No, she won't," Melody dejectedly insisted as Jeff ushered Brandon and Carole Anne out of the clinic.

A very pleased feeling was pouring through her. Carole Anne could feel herself smiling again. All over. "What was that all about? Aunt Connie wrote that Melody was married to Frank Campbell."

"Divorced," Jeff corrected as he headed toward the rear of the clinic where his truck was parked. "Just."

They passed Melody's flaming-red sports car. The woman had done well for herself, Carole Anne mused. "I guess she's set her sights on you as the next victim."

He grinned at her choice of words as he opened the passenger door for Brandon. "Never cared for her very much, did you?"

Carole Anne remembered telling him so once. They had shared a great deal then, she and Jeff. Problems, opinions, dreams. And a friendship that had bloomed.

"Melody always had as much substance as the first coat of nail polish." Even her car reminded Carole Anne of the polish the woman had been wearing. "All she ever cared about in high school was dating and makeup." She frowned, remembering. Remembering, too, that it had annoyed her that all the boys seemed to flock to Melody. Jeff had been one of the few who had been unaffected. "She was so stereotypical, she gave the rest of us blondes a bad name."

"No one could ever give you a bad name." He slid a finger down her nose. It seemed incredibly intimate. The next moment, he was turning toward Brandon. "Up you go." Jeff boosted Brandon into the passenger seat inside the cab of his truck. He turned to look at Carole Anne. "We'll be back about six. That all right with you?"

"Fine." She helped Brandon buckle his seatbelt. "Stay on the bank, understand?"

"Yes, Mom," Brandon answered in a patient, annoyed tone. He wished she'd stop thinking of him as a baby.

She kissed Brandon and shut the door, locking it. She turned and followed Jeff as he rounded the hood. "So, are you seeing her?" She hoped that he realized she was asking the question as a concerned friend and nothing more. Just idle curiosity. Friends had that about each other. Curiosity.

He opened his door. "Who?"

He sounded entirely too innocent, she thought. "Melody."

Jeff stopped to think. "Professionally, she's been in three times."

He was being purposely evasive. Why? Did Melody have her hooks in him? She would have thought Jeff too smart not to see through someone like Melody. Perhaps not. She hadn't seen through Cal until it was too late, she reminded herself.

"And privately?" she prodded.

"Once." He got in behind the wheel. "Dinner and a movie," he recalled. "Neither one of which lived up to my expectations."

She caught the door just as he was going to close it. She wasn't about to let him get away so easily. "And Melody?"

His expression gave nothing away and succeeded in totally piquing her interest. "Melody was exactly what I expected her to be."

She waited for him to elaborate. He didn't. "Meaning?" she asked between clenched teeth. He was doing this to her on purpose.

The grin was slow and sexy, just as he meant it to be. "Didn't Aunt Connie teach you that gentlemen never talk about their dates?"

Her mouth fell open. He couldn't have. Not Jeff. Not with Melody.

Jeff grinned, pulling the door out of her lax fingers. He slammed it soundly. "See you later."

He left her standing in the driveway, annoyed and confused. Annoyed that he wouldn't give her a straight answer and confused as to why his seeing Melody socially should be such a big deal to her.

Carole Anne shut her eyes and could almost see Melody pouring herself out of her dress and all over Jeff.

So what? Jeff didn't mean anything to her *that* way. They were just friends, and if he wanted to keep his dating life a secret, that was fine with her. She'd gone out with a lot of men since Cal had walked out on her.

A lot of men.

And right now, she couldn't recall a single face, a single name. She sighed as she walked along the hot, softening asphalt, her heels leaving small dots in the wake of her footsteps as she made her way to her car. None of them had left any impression on her. As soon as things began to get serious, so did she. She seriously rejected each one of them.

As she got into her car, she saw Melody leaving the clinic, a very angry expression distorting her finely boned face.

Tough luck, Melody. Today he belongs to Brandon.

Carole Anne drove off, whistling.

Jeff brought Brandon to the exact same place he and Carole Anne had been yesterday. To his surprise, it had taken the little boy only ten minutes to settle down. He would have expected the kinetic energy zinging in his veins to last longer. After asking only a handful of questions, Brandon sat down beside Jeff, his pole in his hands, and seriously addressed the task of fishing for their supper.

Brandon watched the end of the line where it entered the water. Nothing had been happening for a long, long time. He wondered if the people who had cleaned out the lake had cleaned out the fish, as well. Aunt Connie wasn't going to be happy. He had promised to bring back a lot of fish for dinner.

He slanted a look at Dr. Jeff and sighed, then resumed staring at the way the sun was glistening on the water, making more colors than he had in his crayon box.

He liked Dr. Jeff because he was fun and because he acted like he was listening to him when he talked. Then Brandon frowned, remembering Kirk. Kirk had been nice, too, until he found out that Mom wasn't going to go away with him on that vacation he'd wanted her to go on.

Brandon snuck another look at Dr. Jeff and wondered if he was in love with his mom.

That was the third time Brandon had looked at him as if he was trying to figure something out. The boy wasn't too shy to ask questions. Why was he suddenly so quiet?

"What?" Jeff prodded gently.

Caught, Brandon shifted restlessly on the grassy bank. "Huh?"

The boy was as good at feigning innocence as his mother, Jeff thought fondly. "You've been sneaking looks at me for a while now. Want to tell me about it?"

Brandon shrugged. He felt funny talking about his thoughts, but he wanted to hear Dr. Jeff tell him that he was wrong to think what he was thinking. He didn't normally like the men who his mother went out with. They usually suggested he go to his room or ignored him as if he wasn't even there. He had thought one was different, but he had been even worse.

Confused, Brandon let out a huge breath. He stretched his feet out in front of him and studied the tips of his sneakers. They were brand new. His mother always made sure he had brand new sneakers. Just when they were getting comfortable, she'd throw them out, saying something dumb like they were wearing out. He didn't much like new sneakers. They pinched.

He looked up and saw that Dr. Jeff was still waiting for him to say something. "How come we're here?"

Jeff caught the pensive, almost defensive note in the boy's voice. Something was up and he was going to have to proceed with caution. Jeff could remember what it had felt like not being taken seriously when he was around Brandon's age.

Jeff nodded toward the lake, knowing that this wasn't what Brandon meant, but he had to start somewhere. "This is where the fish are and I promised you that I'd take you fishing."

It was a nice promise and Dr. Jeff had kept his word. But that still didn't answer the question that was bothering him. "Why?"

Jeff felt like a tenderfoot lost in a dark forest without a compass and no stars to guide him. He felt his way slowly.

"Because I thought you might like to go fishing." Maybe the boy was just being impatient because they hadn't caught anything. Attention spans at this age tended to get used up quickly. "Would you like to go home?"

"No." Brandon turned huge eyes up at him. Had he gotten Dr. Jeff mad? "Unless you do." He peered at the man's face, looking for a clue. "Do you?"

Jeff smiled easily. He was enjoying being here like this. With all his responsibilities, he didn't get much of a chance to relax anymore. He missed it. "No."

The boy still looked as if he was struggling with a problem, something that was troubling him. "Okay, partner, what's bothering you?"

Rather than a question, the words tumbled out in the form of an accusation. "You're just being nice to me to get to my mom."

So that was it. He wondered who had disappointed Brandon in the past. Jeff leaned back and studied the small, serious face. "Figured that one out on your own, did you?" he asked slowly.

Brandon's lower lip trembled a little, and he bit it. "Yeah."

Dr. Jeff wasn't saying no. That meant it was true. He *was* just being nice to him because of his mom. Brandon felt anger welling up inside of him. And huge disappointment. He had no names for the feelings. He only knew he didn't like them. Because they hurt.

Jeff stuck the end of his pole into the ground between his legs, still studying Brandon. His heart went out to the boy. He remembered how tough it had been, growing up fatherless.

"Pretty heavy thinking for a six-and-three-quarter-year-old. Ready for some more heavy thinking?"

Brandon's eyes were wary as he regarded the man beside him. "Like?"

The kid was going to make a good lawyer, Jeff thought. Maybe Harvard. "Like I *do* like your mother an awful lot, but maybe, just maybe, I like you, too."

"Why?"

Definitely a lawyer. Maybe Yale. He'd look into setting up a fund at the bank soon. "Because you're a neat kid."

The description had a familiar ring to it that made Brandon smile. He decided that maybe it was going to be all right, after all. "That's what my mom says."

Jeff thought he felt a tug on his line, but the next moment, it was gone. He grasped the pole in his hands, just in case. "That you're a neat kid?"

The dark head bobbed up and down. "Yeah."

Dr. Jeff's smile was broad and it made him feel good all over. Yeah, things were going to be okay.

Jeff leaned lazily back against the tree. "See, we think alike, your mom and I." He turned his head and saw that the boy had relaxed again. "If I had a kid, I'd want him to be like you."

Brandon's eyes narrowed, searching for the lie. "Honest?"

Jeff held up two fingers in the Boy Scout salute, or what he hoped would pass for the Boy Scout salute. "Honest."

Brandon squirmed a little in his seat. A fly buzzed around his head and he waved it away. "How come you don't have kids?"

Brandon would be disappointed if they didn't come home with a fish. Reluctantly, Jeff rose to his feet and cast out again. "I'm not married."

Brandon emulated Jeff and scrambled to his feet. "You gotta be married to have kids?"

Heavy-duty question, Jeff thought. At six, the most straightforward answers were the best. "I do."

Brandon rolled over Dr. Jeff's answer in his head. It sounded good. Like it would make him safe, he thought. He and Mom had a good deal going, but there were times he missed having a dad like many of the other kids in his school. Mom couldn't pitch worth a darn.

Small blue eyes watched Jeff's face intently. "You wanna marry my mom?"

Jeff laughed. He knew Carole Anne wouldn't appreciate Brandon acting as her marriage broker. If only things were as simple as the way a six-year-old saw them. Say yes and it happened.

Jeff sank down again on the ground, crossing his legs before him Indian fashion. Brandon dropped down beside him, mimicking him move for move. "Yeah, I do. But let's just keep it between us for right now."

But then how could his mother marry Dr. Jeff if she didn't know he wanted to marry her? Brandon didn't understand. "How come?"

He saw Brandon's line grow taut. Jeff placed his hand over the pole to keep it from slipping out of the boy's hands. "Because we don't want to scare away your mother."

Excited, Brandon wrapped his hands around the pole, bracing himself. "My mom's not afraid of anything. Except maybe for spiders," he amended, struggling with the pole. "She pretends she's not, so I don't get scared, but she's got a funny look in her eye when she sees them. Is this a fish?"

Jeff nodded, holding the pole just tight enough to keep it from slipping out of Brandon's hands but not enough to make the boy feel that he wasn't the one landing the fish.

"This is a fish." He looked at the eager young face. "When I marry your mother, we can both protect her from spiders."

Brandon's face split almost in two. Dr. Jeff *was* going to be his dad. "Good deal!"

And the bargain was sealed.

All he had to do now was convince Carole Anne, Jeff thought as he urged Brandon to his feet. Standing behind the boy, he held on to the pole and talked him through the process.

If only landing Carole Anne was this easy, he mused. But he was going to do it, he promised himself. This time, she wasn't going to be the one that got away.

"Bring out your frying pan, Aunt Connie, we're having fish tonight!" Jeff announced in a loud voice as he walked in the back door.

Brandon was almost dancing on his toes as he burst into the kitchen ahead of Jeff. In his hand he held three trout strung together. His trout. He was struggling manfully to keep them from dragging on the floor, but it wasn't easy.

"I caught them all by myself!" Brandon sang out. "Didn't I, Dr. Jeff?"

Jeff was rummaging through the cupboard for something to place the trout on. "You sure did."

Aunt Connie came fluttering in from the living room. Seeing the fish held aloft by her great-nephew, she clapped her hands together as if Brandon had just performed a feat that had never been matched before.

"And here I was, wondering what to make for dinner. You saved the day, Brandon." Brandon beamed proudly as Connie conveniently forgot about the beef Stroganoff she had simmering on the stove.

She took the fish from Brandon just as Carole Anne entered. She had been upstairs, going through an old album of high school photographs she had found, drifting precariously down the river of memories on a raft that wasn't completely waterproof.

Connie elaborately admired the fish, delicately averting her eyes from the glazed orbs. "This will taste delicious." She looked over toward Jeff. "You'll stay for dinner, Jefferson?"

He took the fish from her. Aunt Connie looked relieved, he noted. She was an old dear. "Wouldn't miss it."

Carole Anne arched a brow. Now how did she know he was going to say that?

She hugged her son to her. "Great job," she congratulated Brandon. "Never saw better-looking trout in my life."

"Having a good teacher helped," Brandon said craftily, looking from Dr. Jeff to his mom.

She smelled a rat and wasn't quite sure why. "All right." Carole Anne moved the platter with the trout toward Jeff.

"How about cleaning the fish, since Brandon caught them?"

He took a knife out of the drawer underneath the counter. Grasping it in his hand, Jeff grinned good-naturedly. "Still as bossy as ever, aren't you?"

"It's a dirty job, but someone's got to do it."

Satisfied that she wasn't going to be the one who had to gut and clean the fish, she took Brandon's hand and began to usher him toward the back stairs. Except that he wasn't moving.

"Come on, Brandon, let's get you cleaned up and you can tell me all about the fishing trip."

Brandon looked ready to bust as he shook his head. "Can't."

He'd never kept anything from her before. She looked down at her son. "Why?"

Brandon beamed and snuck a look at Jeff. "'Cause we talked about a secret."

"Oh?" Carole Anne looked at Jeff suspiciously. The innocent shrug he offered only heightened her wariness. Just what had he been filling her son's head with? "What kind of a secret?"

"Carole Anne, I'm surprised at you. If he told you, then it wouldn't be a secret now, would it?" Jeff chided. He didn't bother attempting to keep a straight face.

Brandon wiggled free of his mother's grasp and returned to Jeff's side. "'Sides, I'm gonna help Dr. Jeff with the fish." He squared his shoulders. "I caught 'em, I should be able to clean 'em." He reached for the knife on the counter next to the fish.

Carole Anne was quick to grab it and hold it out of his reach. "Brandon, I don't want you handling a knife."

Very gently, Jeff took possession of the knife. He winked at Brandon, taking care to salvage Brandon's pride. "We'll find something for you to do," he assured the boy. Jeff looked at Carole Anne. "You worry too much."

Oh, now he was getting critical. Well, he had no right to barge into her relationship with her son.

"He's *my* son," she informed Jeff in a voice that told him to back off.

There was something more at stake here than territorial rights. "Yes, but someday he's going to have to be his own man. That doesn't happen overnight."

She understood his implication. But he was on the outside, looking in. Carole Anne opened her mouth to tell Jeff exactly what he could do with his bachelor-hatched philosophy when her aunt took her arm gently.

Carole Anne looked quizzically at the older woman.

"Did I tell you, dear, that I haven't picked out my wedding gown yet?"

Carole Anne blanched, the tug of war over Brandon's education momentarily forgotten. There were exactly thirteen days to the wedding. What was her aunt thinking of?

"What? Do you have any idea how long it takes to order a wedding dress?"

Jeff looked over his shoulder as he placed the cutting board on the counter. "This is Belle's Grove, Carole Anne, not New York."

Connie seemed oblivious to the discussion going on around her. She had a starry look on her face as she envisioned her wedding day.

"I was thinking of something long and flowing," she told Carole Anne. "Emmett likes to see me in beige, but I was thinking of something along the lines of a creamy blue. Or perhaps pearl." She looked up at Carole Anne, using her strictly as a sounding board. "I suppose that white is out of the question."

"If it makes you happy, Aunt Connie," Jeff put in, "go with white."

"Such a dear boy," Aunt Connie murmured. Her voice trailed off as she drifted into the living room.

Carole Anne was about to follow her, panic riddling her soul as she thought of the fact that if she hadn't arrived when she did, Aunt Connie would be cakeless, foodless, and would probably wind up marrying Emmett in her strawberry duster.

She glanced over her shoulder at Brandon.

Jeff had taken out the step stool and Brandon was on the third step. The top of the boy's head barely came up to Jeff's shoulder.

Carole Anne felt a pang. This was how she had once envisioned that things would be, except that it would have been Cal standing like that next to his son, their heads together over some project.

She felt tears gathering in her eyes.

Returning for her aunt's wedding was twisting her emotions up in knots, wringing things out of her she had thought long gone. Or at least, safely buried. Walls had been built up, dams constructed. Being here drove major cracks through all of them.

"Carole Anne?" Connie popped her head back into the kitchen, looking at her niece patiently.

Carole Anne sighed and turned toward the living room. "Coming, Aunt Connie."

Chapter Seven

Connie smiled to herself as she watched her niece leave the table and cross to the sink on the pretext of getting a glass of water. Carole Anne was trying to be as subtle as she could about it, but she wasn't fooling her any. Her niece must have found an excuse to look out that back window half a dozen times in the past twenty minutes.

Good.

Feeling very satisfied, Connie leaned over and squeezed Emmett's hand just as he began to reach for the butter. They exchanged looks, his was tolerantly loving, hers jubilant. Everything was coming along very nicely.

Brandon was plowing through his broccoli like a steam shovel, trying to work his way to the good part. In Brandon's case, the meat loaf. He was a compartmental eater, going from least to most favorite.

Just like his mother had been at that age, Connie remembered, affection spilling through her like honey being poured over a waffle.

"He'll be here soon, dear," Connie told her niece. "Now stop pressing my chintz curtains and come have your dinner before it's stone cold."

Carole Anne looked distracted as she returned to the table. She didn't even bother with the half-empty glass she had brought back with her.

"I wasn't looking for anyone." She scooted her chair under the table. Brandon looked up at her, grinned, and went back to terminating his vegetables. "I just thought I heard a noise in the backyard, that's all." There was silence at the table. Carole Anne pushed on. "Like a stray cat or..."

Her voice trailed off. No one was buying this, not even her six-year-old. She shrugged ruefully as she sank her fork into a mound of mashed potatoes that was slowly growing cold. She settled for a half-truth. "I was just wondering what was keeping Jeff, that's all. He's been over here for dinner every night since I've been here."

It had gotten to the point that she could almost set her watch by him. As soon as the last piece of silverware was set down on the table, the back door would open and Jeff would walk in. And then the kitchen, never a gloomy place to begin with, would brighten twofold. Brandon would come to life with questions and stories, and Aunt Connie would flutter about and fuss.

It was a scene out of a 1930's movie. Hopelessly corny. And yet it seemed to work for everyone. Except her, of course.

"Council meeting, no doubt," Emmett guessed. He delicately wiped his white mustache as he savoured his last bit of apple cinnamon pie. He turned to his fiancée. "I keep eating like this, Constance, they're going to have to let out my tuxedo before the wedding."

"A tuxedo," Connie sighed. "Can't you just see it, Carole Anne?" She smiled into Emmett's eyes like a smitten teenager. "Oh, you'll look so dashing, Emmett."

"Town council?" Carole Anne prodded, completely mystified. Were they talking about the same man? "Jeff's on the town council?"

Saying it aloud brought her no closer to believing it than before. She waited to be contradicted and told that she had misunderstood. In high school, Jeff had almost opted not to graduate because he found the idea of delivering a mandatory senior speech excruciatingly painful. He hadn't wanted to face the class. She had done some persuasive talking of her own at the time to convince him to get through it.

"Why, yes, didn't I tell you?" Connie rose, clearing away her dinner plate as well as Emmett's. "I meant to." She shook her head as she placed the dishes in the sink. "Don't know how that slipped my mind."

Curious, confused, Carole Anne turned to Emmett. The man she had held suspect only a week ago she now regarded as a friend. It had taken her only a little while in the man's company to see that Emmett Carson really did love her aunt. He treated Aunt Connie like a princess and Carole Anne found it incredibly sweet. And unique. She hoped that what they had would last.

God knew it was rare.

Connie brought out a second pie and set it down in front of Brandon. Chocolate mousse was his favorite. He began to eat faster, eager to clear his dinner plate.

Carole Anne groaned as she shook her head. Brandon was on his way to a stomachache. "Is there anything else about Jeff that someone forgot to mention?"

Emmett thought for a moment. "He heads the volunteer firemen."

Connie cut a wedge of chocolate mousse and placed it on Emmett's plate. "And he almost married Sheriff Wade's daughter a year ago last spring." She crossed to the stove for the coffeepot.

Carole Anne looked at her aunt, startled. The information momentarily knocked the air out of her. First Melody, then the town council, now Aunt Connie was telling her that Jeff had almost married the homecoming queen. What had happened to the shy boy she had known? "Josephine?"

Connie brought the pot of coffee over to the table. "Yes, that's right, that's her name. When Jeff called it off a week before the ceremony, that's when I knew."

Aunt Connie had a habit of fluttering around a conversation like a humming bird meandering from flower to flower. Carole Anne's head began to hurt. "Knew what?"

Connie looked at her niece. She never suspected that the girl was slow. Such a surprise. "That he wasn't over you, of course." She smiled conspiratorially at Emmett. "Any fool could see that."

Emmett accepted the hot cup of coffee Connie passed to him. "Let the girl be, Constance," he reproved kindly. "She doesn't need added pressure from us." He smiled indulgently at Carole Anne. "She's old enough to make up her own mind about things. And people."

Carole Anne smiled, grateful for the man's help. Emmett was exactly what her aunt needed, a man who provided gentle, loving guidance.

And who did she need? Carole Anne had no idea. Until she had returned to Belle's Grove, she hadn't thought she needed anyone, now she wasn't so sure.

No, that was absurd. She knew exactly what she needed. Brandon and her career. What she didn't need was to let her mind wander fancifully, considering things that couldn't happen. She had outgrown Belle's Grove and outgrown the belief in living happily ever after. If she were to forsake common sense and marry Jeff, they'd only wind up arguing. They had such different goals in life, such different tastes. Within months, they'd be making each other miserable. Passion wasn't a safeguard or a deterrent. She'd been passionately in love with Cal and look where that had led. To a dead-end street and to her lying alone in bed, crying.

Well, it wasn't going to happen again. Especially not in a tiny town like Belle's Grove. Only fools made the same mistake twice, and she wasn't a fool. At least, not any longer.

There was a light rap on the back door. The next moment it opened and Jeff walked in. He crossed straight to Aunt Connie's chair. Leaning over, he grazed her forehead with a kiss.

"Sorry I'm late." He addressed the words to everyone at the table, but his eyes came to rest on Carole Anne.

Connie was already shuffling to her feet, the meat loaf platter grasped in her hands. "I'll just heat this up for you—"

Jeff gently laid a hand on her arm, restraining her. "Hot or cold, you whip up the best meat loaf in the state." He took the platter from her hands and set it in the middle of the table. "This'll be fine."

Jeff slid into the chair beside Carole Anne. He leaned forward to see around her. "How're you doing, Brandon?"

"I'm great," the boy chirped.

Carole Anne was busy scrutinizing Jeff. "What's that thing around your neck?"

Jeff stopped helping himself to the meat loaf and looked down. He didn't see anything out of the ordinary. "A tie."

She ran a fingertip over it. The light gray tie felt silky. She smiled. He *had* changed. "I don't remember ever seeing you in one."

That was because he had never really felt comfortable wearing a tie, but concessions had to be made sometimes. "The head of the town council has to try to look the part once in a while." Jeff loosened the loop and slipped the tie off over his head. "Saves time," he explained to Brandon. The boy's brows were drawn together in a small vee as he watched him. "This way, I only had to make the knot once."

Carole Anne was still trying to assimilate the first part of his explanation. She felt as if she were Alice, two minutes after the girl had tumbled down the rabbit hole.

She stared at him in disbelief. "Head?" she repeated. "You're the *head* of the town council?"

Jeff let himself savor a bite of dinner first before answering. "Yes, why?"

She now understood what the phrase being knocked over by a feather meant. "When did this happen?"

Jeff shrugged, taking another bite. "I don't know. A year ago, maybe two."

Emmett had a clearer recollection of the event. "Two and a half years ago to be exact," he told Carole Anne. "It was a unanimous vote."

Carole Anne glanced at her aunt. The woman couldn't have looked prouder if Jeff was her own son. Carole Anne shook her head, stunned by the metamorphosis. She looked at Jeff, amused and amazed. "So when are you up for the Nobel peace prize?"

He took the teasing remark in stride. "Maybe in another year or so. I have to work it into my schedule." Jeff finished his serving quickly. He'd been ravenous and the meeting had dragged on and on. "Speaking of schedules—" Jeff glanced at Carole Anne before he took the pie that Connie was pushing toward him "—I'm free tonight."

"What a surprise," Carole Anne quipped.

Jeff had been free every night so far, except for last Wednesday when he had rushed to Larry Moore's house because three-year-old Jennifer had come down with a case of the croup. He'd spent all the other evenings right in Aunt Connie's living room, entertaining Brandon, joining in on making the wedding plans and, for the most part, making himself one of the family.

Except that he wasn't, Carole Anne reminded herself, not part of *her* family at any rate.

"How do you feel about going down to the billiard parlor and playing a game or two?" he asked her between mouthfuls of Connie's pie.

They hadn't been alone together since that afternoon at the lake. It would be a mistake to tempt fate twice, she decided. "I don't think—"

Jeff raised a brow, a cocky smile on his face. "I'll even spot you a few points."

He had tapped into her sense of competitiveness. "Oh, like I need them."

Jeff retired his fork and pushed aside his plate as he shrugged innocently. "I don't know, you might have gotten rusty since I last played you." He leaned forward to look at Brandon again. "I taught your mother everything she knows about pool."

"Don't you believe him, Brandon," Carole Anne warned. "He showed me which end of the cue stick to hit the balls with, handed me the chalk and said good luck." Her eyes narrowed as a confident smile played on her lips. She turned to Jeff. "Okay, you're on." Carole Anne looked at Brandon. "Want to come along and watch him get creamed?"

Brandon very much wanted to go with his mother and Dr. Jeff. But Aunt Connie had told him today that Dr. Jeff had to have some time alone with his mom if she was ever going to agree to marry him.

"Nah, I'm gonna stay here—"

Concerned, Carole Anne felt his forehead. Had his twenty-four-hour bug made a reappearance? "Aren't you feeling well again?"

Embarrassed at being treated like a baby, Brandon pulled his head away. "Aw, Mom, I'm okay. I'm just gonna—play with Jimmy," he finished, proud of himself for coming up with the excuse.

Brandon thought it over. It seemed like a pretty good idea at that. The Jacksons lived on the other side of Aunt Connie's house. There were three kids, two older ones he didn't much like, and Jimmy. Jimmy was his age—almost. He liked Jimmy because Jimmy didn't tell him what to do.

He glanced at Aunt Connie to see if he had done well. He got his answer when she slipped him another helping of pie.

Brandon had already had one piece. Carole Anne frowned at the boy's plate. "He's going to explode, Aunt Connie."

"Look at him eat," Connie pointed out. "Does that look like a boy who's full to you? Let him enjoy himself. He's only young once."

Carole Anne was about to overrule her aunt, but she remembered what it was like, nursing that extra helping of dessert occasionally when she was a child. With a sigh, she retreated.

"If he has a stomachache, you stay up with him," Carole Anne warned her aunt.

"Gladly." Aunt Connie beamed at her great-nephew as the wedge of pie disappeared beneath his swiftly moving fork.

The windows of the billiard parlor always reminded Carole Anne of a church. They framed either side of the front door and were comprised of blue, yellow and green stained glass, depicting the crucial pool tournament scene in *The Hustler*.

Somewhere in the distance, a whippoorwill called, its voice trilling in the night air, competing with a symphony of crickets. Several cars cruised the street, appropriately labeled Main.

It was as if she had never left.

Without thinking, she had hooked her arm around Jeff's as he escorted her away from the truck. She was too busy trying to bank down the wave of nostalgia that threatened to overcome her.

"Nothing's changed," she commented.

Jeff pointed to the bright neon sign overhead that proclaimed Paul's Billiard Parlor. "Sure it has. Paulie finally replaced the bulb in the letter *B*."

"No more 'illiard Parlor.'" She laughed, shaking her head. "Progress."

Jeff held the door open for her. "Things don't always have to change, Carole Anne."

The darkness within the parlor was cool and friendly. Paulie had put in an air-conditioning unit, as well as replaced a bulb, she noted.

"Sure they do. Otherwise, there's stagnation." She looked around. There was a scattering of men inside the parlor. She thought she recognized several of them.

"I tend to think of it as tranquillity." Jeff nodded at the owner as he ushered Carole Anne toward the billiard rack.

A philosopher, as well. She did nothing to hold back the smile she felt forming. "You've come a long way from that stuttering, awkward kid who couldn't make his point on the debating team in high school."

He chose a cue stick and gestured for Carole Anne to select her own. "Mrs. Hinkley stuck me in on the team at the last minute." He laughed disparagingly, remembering how tongue-tied he had been and how miserable. "I think she wanted to lose."

"Well, she did." Carole Anne looked over several cue sticks before taking one.

He was never comfortable talking about himself. "Let's get back to the present." He indicated the only free table. Four others were occupied. "How bad are you?"

She waited as he picked up a rack. "Well, that all depends."

Jeff paused, looking at her suspiciously. "On what?"

She grinned. "On how much you want to wager on the game."

He moved around the table, taking out balls from the pockets. "You thinking of hustling me, Carole Anne?"

She opened her eyes wide, the picture of feigned innocence. "Me?" She placed her hand to her breast the way she'd seen Melody do, and then fluttered her lashes. "Never."

Jeff racked the balls up to the billiard spot. He nodded vaguely to take in the room. "You are the city slicker in this group."

Holding the cue stick and resting one arm on the other, she shrugged. "Like you said, I might be rusty."

Anxious to start now that she was here, Carole Anne began to circle the table. Resting a forearm on the rail, she leaned over and ran the stick's shaft through her fingers. Closing one eye, she pointed the tip of the cue at the white ball.

She glanced over her shoulder at Jeff. "My break?"

He gestured grandly toward the table. "It always has been."

The same look was in his eyes that she had seen at the lake. The same flutter in her stomach rose up in response to meet it.

She forced herself to concentrate on the game, and directed the cue stick. Multicolored balls went flying across the green felt like so many molecules released during an explosion. They announced their presence by colliding with one another and the sides of the table. The one ball flew into the head pocket.

Rusty. In a pig's eye. She'd obviously kept up on the game. Jeff inclined his head when she looked at him smugly. "Nice break."

She circled and chose her next shot. "It gets even better," she promised.

Jeff stood behind her, watching as she stretched over the table. Her denim shorts rode up and hugged her firm posterior in a way that had his mouth going dry. "No argument."

She looked over her shoulder and saw the desire he made no effort to hide. But for some reason, it didn't make her feel nervous. Perhaps because there were so many people around and she could safely banter.

"You're a doctor. You're not supposed to leer."

Jeff took a step closer. His thigh brushed up against her. The safety factor was reduced. "For tonight, I'm the head of the town council, and the head of the town council's allowed to leer."

She laughed and sent the two balls flying into the center pocket.

"Hey, when do I get a chance to play?" he asked as he admired the shot.

She measured her next shot and squinted, judging her chances. "Maybe the next game."

It was close.

She missed her fifth shot and it took a while before she got her turn again. Their highly competitive game drew a crowd. She recognized several more men who had frequented the parlor when she was a teenager. Men who had once regarded her as a mascot. Very quickly, it felt as if she had gone back in time and was playing in the parlor on one of those endless sizzling summer nights, playing Jeff for pennies.

Carole Anne sank her final shot and whooped a war cry as she held up her cue stick in triumph.

"I think I was suckered into this," Jeff pretended to grumble as he took out his wallet and handed Carole Anne five dollars.

The handful of men who rimmed the table applauded amid comments to Jeff that they weren't so sure they wanted to be treated by a man who let a city slicker beat him at what they considered to be a man's game.

Carole Anne slid the money into her pocket. "Play you another, double or nothing." Immensely pleased with herself, she rocked back and forth on her toes, waiting for his answer.

Jeff took the cue stick out of her hand and placed it against the wall next to his own. "I think I've taken enough of a beating from you for one night. Want to go for a walk?"

She wrinkled her nose. The parlor was cool. Outside, the air was sticky and moist, prime mosquito conditions. "It's hot."

Jeff played his ace card. It had always worked when they were younger. "Buy you an ice-cream cone."

She hadn't outgrown it. Ice cream was still her weakness. She grinned. "Deal."

"Chicken," one of the men called to Jeff, chuckling as he and his partner returned to his table.

"I'm going to enjoy giving him his tetanus booster when he comes in next week," Jeff commented, holding the door open for Carole Anne. "You know," he speculated as he followed her out, "by all rights, you should buy me an ice-cream cone. You're the one who won the game."

It took a second to adjust to the temperature change. She didn't feel quite as miserable as she thought. "Sore loser."

"Yes, I am," he said softly.

She looked at him, but he was taking her arm and guiding her down the block to Grady's Candy Store. It was the last shop just before the old apple orchard. Progress hadn't been here to visit, either, she noted, and discovered that she was glad.

The screen door hit a small silver bell that announced their entrance as they walked into the candy store. More memories, Carole Anne thought, looking around. The candy store with its racks of comic books and assorted treats had been a mainstay of her childhood.

The old store looked smaller to her somehow, and the woman behind the counter looked a little more hunched and lost inside her shawl. No matter how hot it was, Mrs. Grady always wore her brown shawl wrapped around her shoulders.

"Mrs. Grady," Carole Anne cried, approaching the counter. "You're still here."

Although she looked a little more gnarled than she had, it was as if the woman had never moved from her chair behind the glass counter in the eight years Carole Anne had been gone.

"Where else would I be?" The voice was dusty and gravelly, as if it was sifted over rocks. "This is my store." Paper-thin hands pushed the glasses higher on her long, skeletal nose. The old woman peered through her bifocals, studying Carole Anne, searching for a name. "You're the Jenkins girl, aren't you?"

Carole Anne smiled. It had been years since she thought of herself as that. A pleasant warmth drifted through her. "Yes."

The woman snorted dourly. "I'm out of pistachio."

Carole Anne's mouth dropped open in surprise. "You remember."

Mrs. Grady was indignant at Carole Anne's disbelief. "Sure, why wouldn't I?" One twisted finger tapped her temple. "Memory's as good now as it's ever been." Relaxing, she smiled, and the wrinkled cheeks rose on cheekbones that nearly came to points. "Got peach. That was your second favorite." Without waiting, Mrs. Grady slowly moved over to the ice-cream vat. Taking the scoop in her hand, she served up one peach cone, one fudge ripple. It took her a while, but they were in no hurry.

Carole Anne exchanged looks with Jeff as she accepted her cone. He appeared to be taking all this in stride. "She's incredible."

"And healthy as a horse." Jeff smiled kindly at Mrs. Grady, then pressed a five dollar bill into the woman's hand. "I'll see you in the office soon."

"No need." She shuffled back to her chair. "Haven't had a sick day since '87. Hey, what about your change?" It was a standard game, but Mrs. Grady felt honor bound to play it. Jefferson Drumm had been playing it for years.

"Just credit my tab."

The bell tinkled again, as if to say goodbye as they walked out. Carole Anne couldn't remember when ice cream had tasted this good.

They drifted toward the orchard and then farther. "Remember when we were little and we thought she was a witch?" Jeff nodded as he bit into his cone. It made going to the candy store almost a dangerous adventure. "Does she wear her shawl when she comes in for examinations?" A little of the ice cream dribbled down the cone. Carole Anne licked it from her fingers.

Jeff had an intense desire to follow the path of the ice cream on her fingers.

"No," he answered seriously. "She had a growth on her back. She used the shawl to cover it."

Carole Anne stopped walking. She turned to look at Jeff in surprise. It had never occurred to her that the shawl was anything other than an eccentricity. "All those years?"

He nodded, leaning against a tree. The night sounds were soothing. He let them waft under his skin, hoping they would cool the fever in his blood. "I convinced her to have the growth removed. I think she wears the shawl now out of habit."

She joined him. "You *have* become a smooth-tongued devil."

He considered her compliment. "That remains to be seen."

She noted the certain light that had entered his eyes. Swallowing, she realized that she had just put her thumb through the side of her cone.

"Oh?" Carole Anne began to lick more quickly, stemming the flow before she had a mess all over her hands. "And what did you have in mind to test your powers?"

He shifted so that he was standing in front of her rather than beside her. "Seeing if I can talk you into letting me sample your ice cream." Jeff inclined his head slightly.

"Oh," she murmured again. It wasn't what she had thought he'd say. But for some reason, the safe feeling was still there. "Sure. You paid for it."

She held up the cone. There was only a smidgen of ice cream left on it.

He moved it aside, his eyes on hers. "No, not on the cone."

She raised her head, her mouth inches away from his. "Then how?"

He dropped his own cone. It landed face down in the grass. Slowly, he threaded his hands through her hair, framing her face. "On your lips."

Her breath was backing up in her lungs, staying there as still as the night air. Her heart was beating a tattoo that drowned out the cricket's serenade. "If it's in the name of research—"

"It is."

"Then," Carole Anne whispered, "I guess I can't refuse."

Chapter Eight

Jeff lowered his mouth to hers, his lips as warm and as sultry as the summer-night air. Gently he coaxed the kiss from her until it flowered, absorbing the rays of desire that were nurturing it.

Startled at the power behind the gentleness, Carole Anne was scarcely aware of the ice-cream cone that slid from her hand to the ground.

Feeling the edges of the rush that was overtaking her, she dug her fingers into his hard forearms, desperately attempting to anchor herself as she stretched into the kiss. Stretched on her toes as she searched for more, for what she knew was lying in wait for her.

She raced toward it, the way an eager child raced toward an incoming wave on the shore, anticipation throbbing in her veins.

The sound of labored breathing penetrated her consciousness. She realized with a vague, distant awareness that it was her own. He made her breathless. With so little effort, Jeff had made her feel as if she would never get enough air.

Never get enough of him.

Jeff moved his head back slightly, his lips still close enough to lightly brush over hers as he spoke. The grin spread from his mouth to hers, lodging itself in her soul.

"Looks like I have a brand new favorite flavor." He flicked the tip of his tongue over her lips and had the pleasure of feeling her shiver against him.

Carole Anne wove her fingers through his hair.

"You talk too much," she breathed. An insatiable hunger spread through her, feeding into her very core like tiny tributaries flowing into a river. She had no idea who this person was, responding to Jeff. She didn't care. "Shut up and kiss me again."

"Yes, ma'am."

Winding his arms around her even tighter than before, Jeff held her against him until it was hard to say where she stopped and he began. It was just the way he felt about her. Carole Anne was part of him, part of his soul, and had always been so.

And would always be so.

Carole Anne felt every single contour of his body, every single desire that pulsed through him. It vibrated all through her, reminding her of how long it had been since she had felt like this, since she had ached like this.

Since she had cared for someone like this.

But even in the throes of this madness, she couldn't allow herself to admit to the word that whispered along the edges of her mind. She couldn't admit, even in the deepest, most secret part of her own being, that she loved Jeff. Like a boxer whose arms were withered and couldn't swing, she couldn't release that emotion, couldn't let it go free even if she wanted to. It had been suppressed for so long, it couldn't emerge into the sunlight even if the door to its prison was open.

And she was still afraid to open it.

Even so, her senses swirled through her mind like a gaucho's bola being twirled with increasing momentum overhead, just before it was released.

When his lips left hers, she felt like a drunkard trying to place one foot before the other, having absolutely no idea what had become of the floor. Her heart was racing so hard against her chest, she was surprised that he couldn't see it.

"Where in heaven's name did you learn this technique, Dr. Drumm?"

Slowly, Jeff ran the back of his hand along her cheek, savoring the silky feel. Savoring the bittersweet ache that held his body captive.

God, but he did want her.

He didn't know how much longer he could hold out and play the waiting game. Sainthood was undoubtedly in store for him if he had to wait much longer.

He smiled to himself as he saw his own desire mirrored in her eyes. Soon.

"No technique. Maybe it's just repression," Jeff told her. "You can hold something back only for so long before it explodes."

Was he telling her that he had been celibate? He was going to have a difficult time convincing her of that, not after things her aunt had said. Not after having seen Melody in action.

Carole Anne pinned him with a look. "Melody didn't act as if you had held anything back that afternoon in your office."

Now his smile spread to include her, as well. He leaned one hand on the bark over her head. "Melody's visit, huh? Has that been bothering you?"

"Maybe."

She didn't like that smug grin on his face. And she didn't want him misunderstanding. She wasn't jealous or anything. She was just curious and he hadn't told her anything that would have alleviated that curiosity.

Carole Anne turned and began to walk slowly, threading her way through the dimly illuminated path. The streetlights only reached so far into the orchard. "It's just that I wouldn't want to see a—"

She searched for the right word. There wasn't one to really describe what he was to her anymore. Nothing seemed right, but she settled on the obvious.

"A friend of mine in her clutches."

An owl screeched as it flew overhead. Jeff chose his words carefully. It was nice to have the shoe on the other foot. "Melody and I went out to dinner and saw a rather poor movie."

Carole Anne shrugged, attempting to seem indifferent. "So you already said." She paused, waiting. He just continued walking beside her. The man was utterly maddening. "And?"

Jeff looked straight ahead, his expression half-hidden by the shadows that played over his face. She couldn't see the humor in his eyes. "And she asked me in for a nightcap."

She would. Acting on reflexes, Carole Anne planted herself directly in his path. "To which you...?" She left it up to him to finish.

"Agreed."

Something sharp rose up to stab her, and sadness flowed out of the wound.

"I see." Suddenly she wished she had the ice-cream cone in her hand again so that she could push it into his face.

Purely adolescent feelings, she chided herself. She didn't want him romantically, why did she begrudge him a relationship—?

The hell she didn't want him romantically, she thought, fisting her hands at her sides.

Carole Anne was surprised when he took one hand in his and slowly pried her fingers apart. She looked at him quizzically.

"No, I don't think you do."

She didn't want vivid details. She didn't want to be that close a friend to him. Not anymore. She shook his hand away. "I really don't think I want you to paint any more pictures for me, Jeff, I—"

He took her hand again, more firmly this time, to keep her from running ahead of him. She appeared ready to bolt.

"You will listen to me," he informed her, "before you run off and get lost in the orchard."

She glared at him and what she took to be his superior attitude. "I will *not* get lost in the orchard. I know this area like the back of my hand," she insisted hotly.

Her temper flared at his careless accusation. But it wasn't his remark that annoyed her. She felt like hitting him for being taken in by the likes of Melody Beauchamp.

Jeff merely shook his head, further infuriating her.

"You used to get lost in your own closet without me. I've never seen anyone with such an underdeveloped sense of direction."

To keep her from trying to flee again, he held her in place by bracketing either side of her, bracing his hands on the apple tree.

She was trapped. Folding her arms in front of her, she looked at him defiantly. "All right, tell me about your sordid little affair."

Threads of moonlight had prodded their way through the trees and whispered along her face. Jeff felt his stomach tightening. "She put on some soft music and offered me a glass of white wine."

Carole Anne shifted, restless, angry with him, with Melody, and with herself for God only knew why. "I thought you didn't like white wine."

She was making him crazy, just being here with him like this. He could smell the soap she used, the light cologne she had dabbed at her throat this morning. Every muscle in his body felt like a tight coil.

"I don't. I also don't like to be blatantly seduced." His eyes skimmed over her mouth, her hair. The pulse jumped in her throat, exciting him. "At least, not by Melody Beauchamp." Jeff feathered a kiss over Carole Anne's forehead and heard her sigh. "I left right in the middle of an overture."

"Classical?" Carole Anne managed to push the word past a throat that was growing tight.

"No, hers. She was trying to unbutton my shirt at the time."

Her heart felt as if it was pounding erratically throughout her whole body. Without completely realizing what she was doing, Carole Anne worked the top button on his shirt free of its hole. "You mean, like this?"

She was making his knees weak. He was grateful that the tree was there to lean on. "A little more eagerly," he said, remembering.

Carole Anne loosened another button from its hole. As the striped shirt parted, she slowly slipped her hand inside. Spreading her fingers almost hesitantly over his chest, her skin tingled as it came in contact with the light sprinkling of hair that dusted his chest.

She looked up into his eyes, mesmerized. "Hussy," she whispered.

Jeff moved closer so that she fit against him as if she was the missing part of his jigsaw puzzle. "That's what I thought."

Blood surging in her veins like waves at high tide, she watched, fascinated, as Jeff brought his mouth down to hers once more. With a little cry, she sealed herself against him, wanting nothing more than to have this moment go on forever.

It couldn't go any further, not if she was to remain unshattered. She knew that. And yet the desire was there within her, strong and hard. The desire to make love with him. With her best friend. With someone she had grown up caring for all her life.

With someone, she realized, who she hadn't known at all.

"I think we'd better stop." Jeff murmured the words regretfully against her mouth. "One more second and Dr. Drumm is going to act in a very unprofessional manner in the middle of the town's apple orchard."

Carole Anne laughed softly and agreed, though reluctantly so. It startled her to realize that. "If this is a sample of your bedside manner, I just may have to get sick before I leave," she teased.

When the words were out, they left a bitter taste on her tongue, like an apple that was too tart.

Before she left.

Carole Anne bit her lip when she saw the look in his eyes.

Jeff pushed the empty feeling that threatened to leak out away. "Any time. You have my number." To punctuate his statement, he couldn't resist one more fleeting kiss. "You always have."

His hands weren't quite steady as he rebuttoned his shirt. "I guess I'd better get you back before Aunt Connie thinks we've run off together."

Carole Anne could only nod as she fell into step beside him. Jeff lightly laid his arm around her shoulders. She pressed her lips together. She didn't quite trust her voice at the moment. She was too busy dealing with a sadness she didn't fully understand.

To keep the nagging doubts at bay that were surfacing with the tenacity of fire ants at a picnic, Carole Anne threw herself completely into helping her aunt deal with the rest of the preparations for the wedding.

Or rather, into taking over the task completely.

To her mounting frustration, each question she asked her aunt only garnered the vaguest of answers. It was becoming increasingly evident to Carole Anne that her aunt seemed to believe that the decorating, the music and the food would all take care of themselves somehow. It was as if Connie expected a magic wand to be waved and everything to be ready on the Saturday that was approaching them with the frightening, increasing speed of a boulder rolling down a mountainside.

Several days into endless lists and telephone calls, Carole Anne began to experience what could pass for a revelation.

Her aunt's behavior was vague, even for Aunt Connie. At first Carole Anne was worried that perhaps old age was creeping up on her aunt's mind in the cruelest, most debilitating of fashions.

But as pieces began to fall together, as each morning and evening ushered in the good doctor to her side at the table, Carole Anne began to realize that there was absolutely nothing wrong with her aunt's mind. If anything, the older woman had grown craftier.

It was all too clear to Carole Anne that her aunt had set all the preparations aside for her to handle so that she would be much too busy juggling things to take note of the fact that her undefended ramparts were slowly, methodically, being breached.

By the aforementioned good doctor.

The woman could have outfoxed Rommel, Carole Anne thought, going down the list of wedding guests who had accepted.

As if on cue, Jeff walked into the living room. A huge box preceded him through the door. He was barely managing to balance it. The box was filled to overflowing with the decorations she had sent him to bring back. Decorations she had personally chosen at Jeanne's Stationery and Party Shoppe this morning.

"Where do you want these?" He turned toward Carole Anne and two rolls of white crepe paper fell out and tumbled over one another to the floor.

Beatrice Hanover, the town's only professional seamstress, was in the middle of the room on her knees, attending to Connie's hemline. The woman had sewn two and a half generations of wedding gowns and had altered Connie's first wedding gown in 1948. Her pinched mouth was full of pins and she frowned over the hem.

At the sound of Jeff's voice, she smiled, pins moving in a jagged line.

She glanced over her shoulder in his direction as the rolls landed on the carpet. "Pretty," she commented, sticking another pin into the creamy beige hem.

It was unclear to Carole Anne if Beatrice was referring to the decorations or to Jeff himself. As she recalled, Jeff had always brought a twinkle to the woman's rather myopic eye.

"Right there." Carole Anne pointed to the coffee table that was already overflowing with lists, magazines and copious notes she had made to herself.

Dropping her pad on her crossed legs, she leaned forward and hastily cleared off an area for Jeff.

With a relieved sigh, Jeff deposited the box on top of two bridal magazines.

Connie was standing perched on a short-legged stool like a pigeon debating flight. She had been slowly turning for Beatrice as the other woman worked. She looked uncertainly now at the two women near her feet for guidance.

"Should he be seeing me like this?" Connie spread her hands and gestured vaguely at the dress.

"Stop fidgeting," Beatrice chided crossly. A pin fell from her mouth. With a huff, she reached for it and stuck it into the pincushion strapped to her wrist.

Carole Anne smiled at her aunt and shook her head, picking up her pad again. "It's only bad luck if the groom sees you, Aunt Connie, not the doctor."

Jeff stuck his hands into his back pockets and looked around the room. It looked as if it was bordering on the edge of chaos. It had a soothing feel to it. "Brandon around?"

The question amused Carole Anne. Jeff looked like an overgrown kid himself, in a T-shirt and jeans, with his hair all tousled as if he had been hurrying to get here. There was a tug at her heart she didn't attempt to analyze. "Why, you want to go out and play?"

"No, but Jimmy and Nicky do." Jeff jerked his thumb toward the door. "They were about to come bursting in here, looking for him." He leaned his lanky frame against a wall, studying Carole Anne sitting amid the mess and thought she looked to be in her element. "I thought I'd do a good deed and spare you by running interference."

"My hero." She fluttered her lashes, then sobered as she thought of the little boys tearing through here while everything was in such an uproar. She'd probably never find anything until two weeks after the wedding. "Thanks." Her gratitude was sincere. "Brandon's upstairs in his room playing with that new electronic game you bought him yesterday."

Carole Anne laid her pad aside and started to rise, but Jeff waved her back. "That's okay, I'll go get him."

She settled down again and watched as Jeff took the stairs two at a time. Why did this feel so right? she wondered, this mom-and-apple-pie type of living? She hadn't a clue. This was exactly what she had chafed against when she was growing up. She had thought of it as being too confining, too dull, too unexciting.

And yet...

And yet she had never felt so content, so excited at the same time. There had never been this sort of duality before, she thought as she remembered the night of the billiard game. Happy and sad, content and aroused.

He was making her crazy.

Carole Anne sighed. When she returned to L.A. next week, she was going to have to seriously reorganize her priorities and get everything back to normal. Until then, she was going to feel as chaotic as this room looked.

A flood of sadness drenched her as she thought of the return trip home.

She frowned and shook it off like a puppy shaking off the rain once it was inside a house. She forced herself to concentrate on getting everyone sanely through the wedding. *That* was her top priority at the moment.

She had just crossed off Aunt Connie's suggestion to order pigs-in-a-blanket as the main hors d'oeuvres when Brandon came flying down the stairs. He took the last three steps in a single leap.

She stopped working to study him.

He was messy now, her perfect little man. She had to admit that it warmed her heart just to see him. She couldn't quite bring herself to believe he was actually racing out of the house to go play with children his own age. It was too good to be true.

She had tried to get him to play with children in the area, but they had always made Brandon uncomfortable.

Not anymore, apparently.

When she examined it, Carole Anne realized that her son's transformation had occurred after his fishing trip with Jeff. Specifically, when Jeff had taken him next door to introduce him to the Jackson boys right after the fish dinner.

Doctor, fireman, head of the town council and miracle worker. Quite a résumé. She decide that she didn't know this man she had grown up with at all.

"Be back later, Mom," Brandon called out over his shoulder.

"Hold it, young man." She tossed her pad aside. "When later?"

"Later later," Jeff answered for the boy.

He crossed the room to Carole Anne. Oblivious to everything but the call of his new friends, Brandon went flying out the front door.

Jeff looked down at her. "Don't you know anything about little boys and time, Carole Anne?"

He offered her his hand. She took it and rose to her feet, still looking at the door Brandon had just sailed through.

"Apparently not, but I know about Brandon. He's like a little efficiency expert when it comes to time. He schedules practically everything down to the minute."

Jeff studied her. "And this didn't worry you?"

"Well..."

Carole Anne trailed off, then lowered her voice. Beatrice was an absolute wizard when it came to a needle, but she plied it only half as well as she did her tongue. Beatrice lived for gossip.

Carole Anne inclined her head toward Jeff. "I guess I was too busy dealing with the guilt of not being able to give him a father."

Jeff decided that the conversation would fare better outside, in the open air and away from eavesdropping seamstresses. He ushered Carole Anne out onto the porch. He heard Beatrice sigh loudly behind them.

The heat of the day had burned off a little, though it was far from cool. Carole Anne leaned against the railing, looking out. In the distance, she saw Brandon playing kick ball with his friends.

Jeff perched on the railing, his attention focused on Carole Anne. His face was deadly serious and his eyes were dark. "That wasn't your fault. Cal walked out on you."

She looked up into the air, avoiding Jeff's eyes. Trying to avoid the blow to her self-esteem that the memory of his desertion always aroused. She blinked, vainly attempting to get her tears to retract. "Not exactly a glowing recommendation, is it?"

"No," Jeff agreed quietly, "not for Cal. But then, he always was kind of stupid."

Jeff got off the railing and stood next to her, impotent anger raging through him at the sight of her tears. "The only one stupider was me, telling him to look after you while I was away."

She sighed, rubbing the heel of her hand against her cheek. It was useless to go over all of this. "I don't want to get into that now." It was time to get back to organizing the wedding. At least she was good at doing other people's weddings, she thought. "I've got too much to do."

Carole Anne turned to retreat into the house. Jeff caught her arm. When she tried to pull away, he only tightened his grasp. She was surprised to see the flash of anger in his eyes a moment before he smothered it.

"Then when?" he demanded softly. "When do you want to get into it?"

Never. Please don't do this to me, don't stir up my regrets.

She'd known for a long time now that she had chosen the wrong man to pin her hopes on, to dream with. And in the past week and a half, she had discovered all over again who the right man would have been.

But it was too late. Too late for a number of reasons.

She suddenly felt very tired.

Carole Anne turned her face up to his as dusk began sweeping long, dark fingers through the town, shutting eyes and murmuring softly. "Jeff, please, nothing's going to be resolved by hashing over old business."

He thought it over for a moment, then nodded. "Okay, then how about going over new business?"

He had something up his sleeve. She knew him well enough for that. And it wasn't innocent, no matter what his expression registered. "Like what?"

"I thought you'd never ask." He grinned at her. "Like this."

Jeff took her slowly into his arms, silencing her protests with a long, sweeping look that slid over her like rich velvet. Carole Anne felt his lips even before he touched her.

He kissed her with all the passion he felt, kissed her until she forgot where she was. Kissed her until she was utterly boneless and fluid in his arms.

Kissed her until she forgot all the carefully laid out arguments she had against this going any further than it was.

It was hard to remember arguments when she couldn't even remember her own name.

In the distance, Brandon stopped running and stared. Dr. Jeff was kissing his mother. Grinning, he let out a war whoop.

It jolted into Carole Anne's system and she all but jumped back, feeling exceptionally wobbly on her legs.

She held a hand to her face, flustered. "I forgot about Brandon."

Jeff wanted to pull her back, but refrained. "Don't worry, seeing his mother in a healthy relationship is very good for him."

But she had broken away and was backing up to the door. "We're not in a relationship, healthy or otherwise, Jeff. We're just friends. Get that? Friends-s-s." Confused, not sure if she was coming or going anymore, trying to hold on to sensibilities that no longer seemed as if they applied, she fairly hissed out the word.

"Right," he murmured agreeably. Jeff slipped an arm around her. "Bosom buddies."

"God, you're just as impossible as when we were growing up." She didn't know whether to laugh or cry, and did a little of both.

"More," he guaranteed. He rubbed a thumb over her lower lip. "To be continued."

She turned and entered the house, slamming the door in her wake.

Jeff only laughed softly to himself. She could run, but she couldn't hide. He'd seen his answer in her eyes, had tasted it on her lips. It told him everything he needed to know.

He turned around and watched Brandon play with his friends, enjoying the innocent sight.

Chapter Nine

It was hard to believe that time was really going by so quickly. Carole Anne sat on the sofa, staring at the clock on the mantel as if that could keep the minutes and the hours from somehow ticking away, spilling like grains of sand through her fingers. She couldn't believe it. It felt as if she had just arrived and here it was, the night before her aunt's wedding.

And two days before she and Brandon would return to L.A.

Everything seemed to be spinning by too rapidly. Carole Anne was having trouble holding on to a single thought, a single moment. There was still so much to do. So much to feel. And so much to think about.

There wasn't enough time, she thought, both relieved and melancholy over the fact. Maybe if she thought things through too hard, she'd make the wrong decision. Maybe she had made the wrong decision years ago.

She didn't know.

A rustling sound ended her meandering thoughts and brought her back to the reality of the moment. And the wedding.

Aunt Connie was spreading her gifts out on the coffee table and along the floor. She seemed content just to look at them, her expression as joyous as a child tumbling into a bountiful Christmas.

Moving heaven and earth, Carole Anne had managed to give her aunt a proper shower this morning. One that seemed to include half of Belle's Grove. The women had left well over an hour ago and Carole Anne and her aunt had just now gotten the house back into some sort of order.

Just in time to begin decorating for the wedding, she thought with a huge sigh. She paused, trying to decide where to place the baskets of Aunt Connie's beloved daisies. Maybe on either side of the stairway, she mused, attempting to envision them there.

She sighed again. There was still so much work to be done, so many details to check on. Drained, she couldn't wait for the wedding to be over.

Yes, she could. Because when it was over, she reminded herself, everything would be over. She had a life to get back to. And it wasn't here.

Connie fingered the satiny nightgown Phyllis Decker had given her. She smiled as she thought of wearing it for Emmett. A thoughtful expression passed over her face as she looked toward her niece. Carole Anne should be making plans like this. Carole Anne deserved this kind of happiness in her life. Happiness that Jefferson could give her...if only she'd let him.

Connie had hoped....

But Connie wasn't giving up yet. There was still tomorrow. Tomorrow. She sighed like a young bride as Carole Anne glanced toward her.

Connie replaced the nightgown and closed the lid over the box. "That was very thoughtful of you, dear, giving me a shower." She ran her hand lovingly over a box that contained a set of bath towels with her initials entwined with Emmett's. "I always love opening presents."

Carole Anne smiled affectionately. When she was growing up, it was hard to decide who took the more childlike delight in Christmas, she or her aunt.

"Yes, I know."

The caterer, Carole Anne thought suddenly. She had meant to double-check to see if there was going to be enough wine. She began to rise, but Aunt Connie laid her hand over Carole Anne's.

"Why don't you put that aside, dear?" Aunt Connie coaxed. She eased the everpresent yellow pad out of Carole Anne's fingers and set it on the sofa beside her. "Relax." Her eyes were kind, and oddly knowing, as if she could read things within her niece's soul that Carole Anne was steadfastly denying. "You seem like the one who's experiencing prenuptial jitters instead of me."

"Are you nervous?" That had never occurred to Carole Anne. She thought of her aunt as being too vaporous and light-spirited to be nervous about the wedding.

But maybe Aunt Connie was experiencing the same emotions that had hit Carole Anne just before she had answered "I do" to that sleepy-eyed justice of the peace that Cal had dragged out of bed.

The memory of her own wedding came flooding back, bringing with it a bitter taste in her mouth. Probably like the one Cal had woken with the next morning. He had married her in the midst of an alcohol-soaked weekend. She had thought at the time that he was just a little high, not drunk beyond remembering. But he had been. She had been too excited to notice. He had taken her breath away, driving over the Nevada state line and straight into Las Vegas.

True, the chapel had been tacky, but her dreams had been powerful enough, hopeful enough, to ignore all that, making the surroundings not quite real to her.

Only later did she realize that it had been her dreams that weren't real.

Aunt Connie laughed softly. "My land, no, child. I've known Emmett a long time now. I'm just excited, not nervous." Her hand still covering Carole Anne's, Connie leaned over and whispered, as if Brandon wasn't old enough to hear, "The dear won't tell me where we're going on our honeymoon." She beamed. "He just says to pack light clothing."

Carole Anne laughed. Her serious memories faded like invisible ink drying upon a page. "Aunt Connie, that could be practically anywhere this time of year, except perhaps Australia."

The information didn't dampen the older woman's enthusiasm in the slightest. "Yes, I know." She took out a silver-plated frame and admired it. This one would hold her wedding photograph. "But that does give it just a tinge of the mysterious, don't you think?" She cocked her head, glancing at Carole Anne, reminding her of a tiny snowbird.

Carole Anne sighed and found herself wishing for the first time that she could be more like her aunt.

"You know, you really are a dear, Aunt Connie. I've never known anyone who gets such pleasure out of doing nothing more than breathing."

And it was true. It didn't take any more than that. She'd never even seen her aunt angry or depressed. The closest had been when her aunt had attended her parents' funeral. And even then, she had maintained a smile for Carole Anne's benefit.

Connie didn't see her behavior as being unusual enough to warrant comment. She had a very basic, simple philosophy that she had always adhered to. Moving the boxes aside, she took her niece's hands in hers.

"Life's a gift, Carole Anne. You don't undermine a gift by looking for the faults in it. That would be rude. You just enjoy it."

She smiled affectionately at the girl she regarded as a daughter. She wished there was something she could do to make Carole Anne happy, to make her forget the pain that Connie saw reflected in the girl's eyes.

"And if it doesn't fit you, or suit your needs at the moment, you discover something about it that does please you." The kindly hazel eyes grew serious. "It's the only way."

Carole Anne had no idea why she suddenly felt like crying. Maybe it was the upcoming wedding. Maybe her emotions were exhausted by being constantly under siege. "You're absolutely right."

Connie squeezed Carole Anne's hand before releasing it. "I've enjoyed having you here, Carole Anne." She looked over toward Brandon. He was lying on his stomach on the floor, the electronic game clutched in his hands, absorbing all of his attention. "Both of you."

Carole Anne noticed with relief that her aunt didn't ask her to stay or even comment on the fact that she was leaving the day after tomorrow. For Aunt Connie, it was this moment that counted, nothing else. No plans for the future beyond the very basic notion that the future would eventually be here and so would she.

That used to annoy her, Carole Anne thought. She remembered straining at the bit to leave this small, insignificant, claustrophobic town. Funny, now that she had returned, she could see the beauty of life in Belle's Grove, the beauty of not rushing about trying to keep up with the madding crowd. If asked, Carole Anne had to admit that she enjoyed being in Belle's Grove this time around. Having gone over the rainbow, she now appreciated the fact that what was here was as unique, as individual, as snowflakes.

And her aunt, Carole Anne realized, was truly a diamond in the rough. At times like these, Aunt Connie would say something incredibly intuitive and sparkle in such a manner that she would take Carole Anne's breath away.

She leaned over and squeezed her aunt's hand. "Me, too, Aunt Connie. Me, too."

The knock on the front door interrupted the moment. Brandon, still holding on to his game, scrambled up quickly. He raced to the door before Carole Anne had a chance to even get to her feet.

"Maybe that's somebody," he shot over his shoulder hopefully.

"It usually is." Carole Anne laughed.

She sank back down into the soft cushion. She was just getting used to feeling secure about allowing Brandon to open the door on his own. Back home, she didn't let him answer the door unless she was standing right over him. The danger of admitting strangers, of talking to strangers, had been impressed upon Brandon since he was a baby. Here, there were no real strangers.

"Hey, Aunt Connie, it's Uncle Emmett," Brandon announced, stepping back to let the man enter.

"Not yet." Emmett smiled fondly at the boy. "But almost."

Brandon began to close the door, but met with resistance.

"Hey, wait a second."

The boy swung the door wide open again as he recognized the voice. "Dr. Jeff!"

The enthusiastic greeting brought a wide grin to Jeff's face. Adulation was hard to resist.

"Hi, Brandon." He looked over Brandon's head and nodded at Carole Anne and Connie. "Ladies."

"Uh-uh." Carole Anne exchanged glances with her aunt, then rose to her feet. "He's being formal." She crossed to where Jeff was standing. "Trouble?"

He shook his head tolerantly. "Such a suspicious mind. No." Jeff slipped his arm around her waist and noted with pleasure that she neither stiffened nor moved away. He wondered how much further he would have to break down her walls before she could walk over them of her own volition. "But Emmett insisted we stop here first."

Carole Anne looked from Jeff to Emmett for a clue. "First?"

"Before we go to his bachelor party," Jeff explained, releasing her. "Nothing like having a traditional wedding with all the trimmings." Carole Anne didn't miss the meaningful look he slanted her. He picked up a party favor that lay on its side on the coffee table and twirled the tiny umbrella between his thumb and forefinger. "How was the bridal shower?"

"Just wonderful. Look at all these wonderful things we got, Emmett." She tilted the lid of the negligee box, letting him look inside. Emmett's face lit up like the sky during a Fourth of July fireworks display.

"I'm looking forward to getting a closer look at that one." Emmett sat down on the edge of the sofa for a moment, taking Connie's hand in his. "I just wanted you to know that I'll be thinking of you the entire time I'm at the party."

It had never occurred to Connie to think anything else. Jealousy was an emotion that her body had never harbored nor even acquired. "Of course, you will, dear. I know that." And with that, she gave him her blessings to have a good time.

Well, Aunt Connie might be completely devoid of any distrustful thoughts, but Carole Anne's interest was definitely aroused. "Just what kind of a party is this going to be?" She leveled a suspicious look at Jeff.

He merely grinned innocently in response. "The usual kind."

Perhaps the grin was a tad *too* innocent. "I've never been to a bachelor party," Carole Anne pressed. "Just what is considered 'usual'?"

He shrugged, enjoying himself. "Food, stories, a little entertainment."

Her eyes narrowed. She could just envision a girl jumping out of a cake and twirling tassels for all she was worth, dressed in barely a smile.

"How little?" By the amused look on Jeff's face, Carole Anne realized she was making noises as if she was a suspicious wife. She backed off self-consciously. "Just curious, that's all."

"Medium little." Jeff attempted to pull his mouth into a straight expression and almost succeeded. The mischievous look in his eyes had her totally unconvinced.

Brandon figured he'd been quiet long enough. He placed himself between Dr. Jeff and his mother. "Can I come, too?"

Jeff looked down at the boy's hopeful face and immediately felt a sharp pang of guilt. He had overplayed this for Carole Anne's benefit. He hadn't meant to arouse Brandon's interest, as well.

"Well, it's not really the type of party you would like," Jeff hedged slowly. "It's strictly a bachelor party."

"But I'm a bachelor." Brandon cocked his head, a little uncertain. "Those are the guys that aren't married, right?"

"Right."

Trapped, unwilling to hurt Brandon's feelings by leaving him out, Jeff searched for a solution. As best man, he was in charge of Emmett's party. It certainly wouldn't look right for the best man not to attend. Still, Brandon's ego was a frail one that he had coaxed and nurtured along these past two weeks. He didn't want to do anything to jeopardize his headway.

Brandon rocked on his toes, impatient. "So, why can't I go?"

Jeff glanced at Emmett. The man was a lanky six three. "It's only for tall bachelors. Over six feet," Jeff informed him. It was flimsy as hell, but it was all he had. He saw Carole Anne roll her eyes behind her son.

"Oh." Brandon's shoulders fell as he tried to deal with the rejection. He didn't think Dr. Jeff would keep him out of something on purpose. Still, it bothered him.

Brandon stared down at his shoelaces and wished he could disappear through the floor. "I just thought...I mean, I wanted to go with you, but..."

Jeff couldn't bear the desolate look on his small face. "Tell you what." Jeff dropped down on his heels, squatting beside Brandon. "You round up Jimmy and anyone else you want to come along, and after I get everything set up at the tall bachelor party, I'll come back for you and the guys. We can have our own bachelor party. Just short guys." He rose again. "Nobody over five feet."

Brandon looked up at Jeff curiously. Dr. Jeff looked like he was a lot taller than five feet. "But you are. How come you can come?"

Carole Anne looked at Jeff with a let's-see-how-you-get-out-of-this-one look.

He didn't even need a second to think. "Because I'm the official bachelor party coordinator."

Slippery as dish-washing liquid, Carole Anne thought in admiration. When had he learned to think so well on his feet? The old Jeff she knew would have never been able to come up with any of these excuses.

Jeff's answer was good enough for Brandon. "Okay, I'll get 'em. When will you be back?"

"We'd better get going." Jeff took Emmett's arm and ushered him from the sofa. If they didn't leave soon, they were going to be late. "Give me about an hour to an hour and a half," he told Brandon. "And we'll hold our party at Grady's Candy Store."

The boy nodded, then scooted out the door ahead of Jeff to tell his friends about the party arrangements.

Carole Anne followed the two men out. She leaned against the screen door, watching Brandon take a hedge in a single leap. She never knew he had that much stored-up energy inside, she thought with a smile.

She glanced at Jeff. "Good thing you're not related to Pinocchio. I don't think you could make it to town from here without having your nose get in the way."

He raised a brow. "Are you insinuating that I told a lie?"

"I don't think 'insinuating' has anything to do with it." Still, how could she find fault with his methods when her little boy looked so happy? She was just glad that Jeff had become so quick. "I suppose you call that more creative fabrication."

Emmett had slipped into the passenger side of Jeff's truck. They had to get going, Jeff thought. Still, he lingered long enough to quickly brush a quick kiss on her lips, tantalizing them both. He grinned. "You're learning."

With that, he hurried down the front steps to the waiting truck.

"No, I'm not," she whispered. She laced her arms around her as if to hug herself, as if to keep something at bay. "If I had learned anything, I wouldn't be feeling this flip-flop sensation in my stomach every time you kissed me."

With a sigh, she turned and went into the house. There was still a ton of work to see to. The house had to be decorated. She had to decide where the tent was going to be set up in the backyard and where to place the flower-woven trellis beneath which the minister would stand. Then there were the flowers themselves. She had to figure out where the carnations were going when they arrived tomorrow morning. The florist had promised to have them all here by six.

She had her doubts about that.

She had her doubts, she thought as the screen door closed behind her, about a lot of things.

Carole Anne tried not to pay attention to the rhythmic kicking against the sofa. Jimmy Jackson was dangling his long legs over the side, bored. Marking time. His cousin

Nicky popped another candy into his mouth as he rocked beside Jimmy on the sofa. Brandon kept watching the front door expectantly.

The television set was on and Carole Anne had popped a popular children's movie into the VCR she had sent Aunt Connie for Christmas last year. No one was watching.

"So when is Dr. Jeff supposed to be coming back?" Jimmy asked.

Brandon sighed, trying not to look as if he was worried. "Soon."

Nicky shook his head, his curly brown hair bobbing about his round face. He looked at his friends importantly. "My big brother had a bachelor party last year when he got married, and he didn't come back until just before the wedding. Aunt Becky was real mad at him."

I'll just bet she was, Carole Anne mused silently.

Jimmy took another handful of silver-wrapped chocolate candy and rose decisively to his feet. He looked at his cousin. "Maybe we should go home. Dr. Jeff probably forgot about coming back."

"No, he wouldn't do that." Brandon looked over his shoulder to where his mother was sitting. There was a plea for help in his eyes.

Carole Anne hadn't been working on her notes for the past fifteen minutes. Covertly she had been sneaking glances at her watch, silently agonizing right along with Brandon.

Jeff was more than twenty minutes late. No doubt he'd forgotten all about his promise to her son. By now, the "little" entertainment he had booked had obviously gotten under way and he had lost track of time.

Well, she didn't have time to worry about Jeff being mesmerized by an overdeveloped body in an underdeveloped costume. She had an unhappy little boy on her hands. Carole Anne glanced at the other two faces. Three of them, she amended.

She placed her pad on the table and rose. "Listen, boys, why don't *I* take you to Grady's Candy Store?" She looked from one boy to another. "Sundaes all around," she announced. "We can still have the bachelor party."

The boys looked unconvinced. "But you're not a bachelor," Jimmy complained. He looked her up and down as if to verify his proclamation. "You're a girl."

She was ready for that one. Placing a hand on the boy's shoulder, she leaned down to Jimmy's level. "A bachelor is an unmarried person, and I'm an unmarried person."

There was something wrong with that reasoning, but Jimmy wasn't quite sure what it was.

Brandon felt a little gloomy over being abandoned by Dr. Jeff, and in front of his friends, too. But at least this helped to save the day. He didn't want to be teased by the others, especially not Jimmy. He was supposed to go over to Jimmy's house tomorrow for a sleep-over and he didn't want to spend the whole time being laughed at for making up stories about Dr. Jeff.

"Okay," Brandon said brightly. "Sounds like a good deal, huh, Nicky?"

Nicky didn't care what kind of a deal it was as long as he got to eat ice cream. He nodded vigorously, scrambling out of the depths of the sofa and onto his oversized, sneaker-shod feet. "Sure."

Brandon was about to say something to his mother when a noise caught his attention. He immediately darted back to the window. "Hey, wait, there's a car."

"Sweetheart," she chided gently. She refrained from taking him away from the window. "There are lots of cars, even here." Carole Anne couldn't help smiling at her own wording.

But Brandon didn't turn around. He lifted the opaque white curtain beneath the drape, peering out. "No, that sounds like Dr. Jeff's truck," he insisted.

She couldn't let Brandon do this to himself. She was wrong to have come here, wrong to let her son get so attached to someone besides her. She was the only person Brandon could ever depend on.

She crossed to the window to draw him away. "Honey, we can't—"

Carole Anne stopped as she saw Jeff's truck pull up in front of the house. A moment later, Jeff stepped out.

Finally, she thought. Still, she had to admit that she was more than a little surprised to see him return.

Jeff hurried up the front steps, aware of the faces in the window. He thought of how nice it felt to have someone actually waiting for him. It was a feeling he meant to perpetuate on a permanent basis as soon as possible.

The door opened for him before he had a chance to reach it.

Three little boys surrounded him. "Sorry I'm late, men. We had a little problem with the caterer." He looked over Nicky's head at Carole Anne. "I sure hope they've got their act together by tomorrow." The little boys had him cornered. No one moved, and subsequently, neither could he. "Nice to have a welcoming committee." He grinned at Carole Anne. "You can close your mouth now, Carole Anne."

The boys, including Brandon, giggled at Jeff's comment.

Carole Anne cleared her throat, giving him a mystified look. "You came back."

He looked at the wreath of smiles around him and felt good. "I said I would."

"Yes, but—" Carole Anne looked at the three faces turned toward them, taking in every word, and decided that she wanted a little privacy. "Excuse me boys, I want a word with Dr. Jeff."

Arm hooked through his, she ushered Jeff aside on the porch and lowered her voice. "I don't understand. Why did you leave the party?"

He didn't see the problem. "I thought I just told you. Because I said I would."

No man was that good, not even Jeff. "Didn't the stripper arrive?"

The woman was downright adorable when she was pretending not to be jealous. "What stripper?"

She fisted her hands at her waist. He was enjoying himself, putting her through this. "Isn't there always a stripper at bachelor parties?"

He laughed, and lightly placed his arms around her. "You've been watching too many movies. I hired a country and western band for Emmett." He had an overwhelming urge to nuzzle her, but resisted. There were too many short witnesses in the area.

"Of course," his eyes twinkled, "it's an all-girl band and they're naked, but I thought—"

Carole Anne punched his arm, but she was laughing as she did it. He was having fun at her expense, but he had returned for Brandon's sake and she loved him for it.

The word echoed through her mind and she was horrified.

"Boy, you still pack a wallop, don't you?" He rubbed his arm. He noticed the sudden change in her expression, but pretended not to. "What are you so upset about? Like I told you at the lake, I wouldn't see anything I hadn't seen before."

She didn't love him. She didn't. At least, not *that* way. Just as a friend. Why was this anxiety attack setting in? She didn't need this now. Or ever.

Carole Anne tried to get her mind back on the topic. "You were leering at me at the billiard parlor, remember?"

He shrugged innocently. "Slight lapse, that's all."

She shook her head, surrendering. "Well, at any rate, they've been watching the clock like little hawks." She nodded toward the boys who were shifting from foot to foot, waiting.

He laughed, rejoining the pint-size group. "I kind of figured that."

She mussed her son's hair and he gave her what he hoped passed for a grown-up look of annoyance. "You'd think they'd never had ice cream before."

Jeff remembered very clearly what it was like to anticipate going to the ice-cream parlor. It had been an occasion for him as a young boy. "You can do something a hundred times, but special circumstances make it unique."

Maybe so. She was willing to agree to almost any of his reasoning now that he was here. She pushed open the screen door. "Well, I'll just get my purse—"

Jeff caught her hand, stopping her. "Sorry, but you're not invited."

She stared at him. "What?"

Jeff remained firm for the sake of the boys. If she came along, he might not be able to give them the attention they deserved and needed. Carole Anne could distract him the way nothing else could.

"This is an exclusive bachelor party." He looked at the group behind him. "Right, men?"

"Right," they chorused, their high-pitched voices raised.

"Besides—" he pretended to look her up and down "—you don't fit the gender requirement or the height requirement." He grinned. "Sorry."

Brandon sidled up to Jeff. "Yeah, sorry, Mom. This is guy stuff."

Carole Anne raised a brow. She could certainly use the peace and quiet to catch up on last-minute details and to make a few more phone calls. Still, she didn't know if she liked being left out of her son's life this way.

"Well, all right, but don't—"

She couldn't continue with her instructions because Jeff had placed his finger to her lips. She stared at him, stunned.

"Don't worry so much." Jeff knew Carole Anne was about to give Brandon some last-minute instructions. He also knew that it would make the boy wince uncomfortably in front of his friends. "He's a sensible guy, Carole Anne." As cover, he added, "They all are."

"Right," the boys sang out again, pleased.

She could only shake her head. Kids got carried away at the earliest opportunity. She was probably going to have to contend with a green-at-the-gills little boy tonight. "All I can say is, boy, do you have a lot to learn about children and parenting."

"I'm always eager to learn, Carole Anne." He herded the boys in front of him. "I'll be back later. Maybe then we can have our own party and you can teach me something."

She sincerely doubted it. It looked to her as if Jeff had learned it all.

"Or," he suggested, running a finger down her nose and then her lips affectionately, "maybe we can play doctor and I can teach you something."

Her mouth tingled and the sensation was echoed through her body. Nervously, she gestured toward the boys waiting at the bottom step. "Your public is waiting, Dr. Jeff."

"For now." Jeff looked at her significantly. "But our time's going to come, Carole Anne."

She had an eerie feeling, as she watched him usher the boys into his truck, that he was right. And she didn't know if she was happy about it.

Or sad.

Chapter Ten

Carole Anne was thoroughly convinced that if she had been born triplets, there wouldn't have been enough of her to go around this morning.

She felt as if she had hit the ground running at four in the morning, after having stayed up late the night before to finish decorating the house. Brandon had fallen asleep, curled up on the sofa, waiting for her to complete tacking up the crepe streamers. Exhausted, she had carried him upstairs and put him to bed around midnight.

It felt as if she had just placed her head on the pillow when the alarm exploded, announcing that it was time to get up again. Wearing a baggy, washed-out T-shirt and frayed denim shorts, praying that her hair wouldn't frizz uncontrollably, Carole Anne had overseen everything and everyone who came within three yards of the house from dawn on.

She had just finished admitting the caterers through the back door when she heard a loud commotion coming from outside the front of the house. Afraid to hazard a guess as to its source, Carole Anne rushed through the living room to see what was going on. It was way too early for the guests to arrive and the florist had just left—again—after rectifying an oversight in the delivery. The people assembling the huge tent for the reception were out back, not front.

Out of the corner of her eye, she saw her aunt drift down the stairs as she hurried to the window. Aunt Connie was still wearing her strawberry duster and looked miles away from being ready. The wedding was in two hours.

Carole Anne drew aside the curtain and looked out, braced for anything.

Or so she thought.

She stared, speechless for a moment, before turning to look incredulously at the woman behind her. "Aunt Connie, there's a man in a truck unloading cages with birds in them on the front lawn."

Connie joined her at the window, peered out, and then moved aside, completely unfazed. "Oh, those are from the next town."

Aunt Connie sounded as if having cages full of birds delivered was an everyday occurrence. Carole Anne followed her away from the window. "They're tourists?"

"No, darling, they're doves."

"Doves?" Carole Anne repeated dumbly. *Doves?*

Aunt Connie smiled tolerantly at her only niece. "You know, pretty white birds," she prompted. "The ones they're always drawing on wedding cards." Connie inclined her head, taking another quick peek out the window. "I've always dreamed about having a flock of doves released over my head just as I said 'I do.'" Connie pressed her lips together, studying Carole Anne. The poor dear looked as if all this was too much for her. "Did I forget to tell you about the doves?"

Carole Anne sighed, searching for patience. "Yes, you did." She tried once to appeal to the woman's reason.

"Aunt Connie, doves are only pigeons in white face. I really don't think—"

Her protest washed over the woman, unheeded, unnoticed. "They'll look so pretty, and Richard assures me that they're all trained." She noted the blank look on Carole Anne's face. "Richard. The man who owns the doves."

She knew that look on her aunt's face. There was no talking her out of this. "I'd feel a whole lot better if he assured you that they were all housebroken." *Doves yet.* "Doves it is." Resigned, she scribbled a note to herself on page two of the clipboard to signal the release of the doves at the proper moment.

Flipping the page over, she looked at her aunt. "Any more surprises I should be ready for?"

Connie thought, then looked at Carole Anne, the soul of innocence. "None that I know of."

"Thank God," Carole Anne muttered to herself. "Shouldn't you be getting ready?"

Connie looked at her watch, then at her duster. "I suppose so." With unhurried steps, she made her way to the stairs.

Brandon appeared on the landing, holding his suit on a hanger like an exterminator holding a rodent aloft. "Mom, do I have to wear a suit?"

Carole Anne stopped in midflight. Now what? "You always wear a suit to parties."

Brandon exchanged smiles with his great-aunt as she moved past him on the landing. He looked down at his mother with the air of someone who was smug in the knowledge that he was right. "I didn't wear one to the party last night."

"A candy store doesn't count." Brandon set his little mouth firmly. Why did he have to choose this moment to test out his independence? It was all Jeff's fault. Jeff. Carole Anne seized her ace card and played it. "Dr. Jeff will be wearing one."

Brandon's attitude did a complete U-turn right in front of her eyes. "Okay." Careful not to drag his suit along the floor, Brandon scooted back to his room.

Carole Anne could only look up toward heaven and shake her head. She and Brandon were going to have to sit down and have a serious talk once this was all over with.

There was an ominous crash from the back of the house.

If this was ever over she amended, hurrying to the kitchen. Aunt Connie might be going on her honeymoon later today, but after this, *Carole Anne* was the one who was going to be in desperate need of a vacation.

She burst into the kitchen. Three middle-aged women, who she had known most of her life, and who had joined forces several years ago to form Belle's Grove's leading and only catering service, were busy milling around the kitchen, fussing over wine and hors d'oeuvres.

Nothing looked amiss here. The crash had to have come from the backyard. Carole Anne flashed a spasmodic smile at the three women as she hurried through the back door.

And then she saw it.

The tent was a huge pool of white on the lawn. The tent that was supposed to be standing by now.

She shut her eyes and counted to ten before venturing any farther. Taking a couple of cleansing breaths, she hurried down the steps to the three men who were gathered about the tent like comrades about a fallen soldier.

She looked at the man closest to her, a man whose forearms were larger than her waist and who looked as if he could walk into a brick wall and keep on walking. She tried to keep the desperation out of her voice. "What happened, Ham?"

Hamilton Fraser looked eye to eye with Carole Anne and shrugged mile-wide shoulders. "Pole collapsed."

Obviously. She bit her lower lip, wondering if the two hundred guests would wilt without the shade of a tent to retreat to. "Is it planning to do that again?"

Ham looked at the other men, then back at Carole Anne. His eyebrows formed a single, dark straight line across his wide nose. "No, Carole Anne, poles don't plan things."

There was no need to take her case of nerves out on him, she thought, upbraiding herself. "Can you get it up in time for the ceremony?"

"Never ask Ham a loaded question like that."

Carole Anne swung around and almost hit Jeff in the stomach with her clipboard. He moved aside just in time. But nothing wiped away the grin on his face. Carole Anne had to be careful who she fed straight lines to, he thought. "You might get more than you bargained for."

She sighed so deeply she would have been able to blow out fifty candles on a birthday cake. "I already have." She hugged the clipboard to her, wishing she could just twitch her nose and make everything fall into place. "This wedding is making me a nervous wreck."

Jeff nodded agreeably. "Fine, we'll elope."

Carole Anne gritted her teeth together. He knew perfectly well what she was talking about. "Aunt Connie's wedding."

His eyes held hers. "That's right, you did that the first time."

She'd had enough. "Jefferson Hewitt Drumm, if you can't help, go away."

"Okay." He laughed good-naturedly as he held his hand up. Carole Anne was obviously a damsel in distress. A damsel who would bite his head off if he didn't take her seriously. "What do you need?"

Carole Anne looked around at the tables that had yet to be brought out, much less covered, the tent that was in a state of collapse at her feet, and the thought of the cages of doves deposited all over the front lawn. This wedding was never going to go off on schedule. "Another week."

Jeff's eyes brushed along her face so intimately she could have sworn she felt the stroke physically. "Yeah, me, too."

For the first time this morning she felt as if time stood still. It was as if she was trapped within one of those slow-motion scenes in a movie and someone had hit the pause button.

This was not the time or the place. Perhaps no time was. She licked her lips. "Just help Ham put up the tent, will you?"

There were things he would have much rather done. Things alone with her where no one could see them. But compromises had to be made. There was a wedding to get under way.

And there was always later. "Sure."

"Thanks." She was halfway across the lawn to the back door when she suddenly came to a skidding halt and hurried back to Jeff.

He turned just in time to see her approaching. He thought about finding ways to keep her perpetually barefoot. Up to the neck.

"Where are your clothes?" she demanded, and heard the other men chuckle under their breath.

Jeff made an elaborate show of looking down at his torso. "Right here, why?"

She was absolutely in no mood to be teased. "I mean, for the wedding. You're not going to be best man in jeans, are you?" She couldn't predict anything about Jeff anymore.

Jeff almost laughed out loud at the small wail in her voice, but knew she would hand him his head if he did. "Boy, you really crack under pressure, don't you?" He saw her eyes grow stormy, and quickly added, "My suit's in a garment bag in the spare bedroom." He arched an inviting brow. "Maybe you'd like to help me into it later."

"Into the garment bag?" She purposely misunderstood his meaning. The men around him, guys she'd grown up with, were hanging on every word. They were now laughing at Jeff's expense. "Count on it. Especially if you don't get that pole up in time." She pointed toward the tent, then pivoting on her bare heel, she was off again.

"That is one frazzled lady," Ham commented. Grabbing a corner of the tent, he moved it out of the way.

Jeff indulged himself and watched Carole Anne's hips sway slightly as she hurried to the house. "I'm counting on helping her unfrazzle later."

The man next to Ham located the fallen pole. "Still have a thing for her, don't you?"

Jeff turned, ready to work. "Always have, always will. Let's see you put some energy into your arms instead of in flapping your lips around, Ham. We need to get this tent up before she comes back out and has a fit."

"You're the doc." Ham put his back into it as he grabbed the base of the pole. The others gathered behind him, pushing upward.

Carole Anne heard the round of cheers as the pole was secured. One problem down, two hundred to go, she thought, making a check mark on her pad.

Somehow, within the next two hours, chaos arranged itself into some sort of semi order. But nothing, it seemed, was destined to go off on schedule. The groom arrived too early. The minister arrived later than he had promised. Both gave Carole Anne cause for concern.

Carole Anne was now dressed in a knee-length pink chiffon matron-of-honor dress that swirled around her with each move she made. Still sporting her clipboard, she was everywhere. One by one, things were falling into haphazard place as she checked them off and wrote more notes in her margins.

Jeff collided with her in the kitchen doorway. He was wearing a pearl gray suit with a light blue shirt. Looking at him, Carole Anne felt her pulse speed up a little. She attributed it to the fact that she had been racing around for hours now.

He steadied her, his eyes washing over Carole Anne in admiration until they came to rest on the clipboard. "I'm beginning to think that thing's a permanent part of your anatomy." It was between them and Jeff gently moved it aside. "I can have it surgically removed if worse comes to worst." His eyes sparkled, teasing. "It might tend to get in the way."

She didn't have time for this, not now, not ever. But especially not now. The house was overflowing with guests and there were just fifteen minutes left before the ceremony. She hadn't checked on Aunt Connie in more than an hour and had a horrid vision of the woman still sitting on her bed in her slip.

Carole Anne wrapped her fingers around the clipboard possessively. "Not if I need something to hit you over the head with." She looked toward the side bedroom. "Is Emmett ready?"

He liked the slight breathless tone in her voice. He would have liked it even better if he had been the cause of it. "He's been ready since this morning." Jeff ran the tips of his fingers along her cheek. "Some of us have been ready longer than that."

Carole Anne could feel herself begin to drift. How could a man's fingertips be so damn seductive? She had to keep her mind on what she was doing. She backed away and almost collided with the tray of hors d'oeuvres set up on the table.

"This is no time to get into a long discussion."

His hands were on her shoulders again, holding her in place. "Fine," he conceded. "'I was wrong' is a very short statement."

"You were?" Despite the fact that she was running out of time, Carole Anne wondered just what he was up to. Was he saying that he was wrong about them?

She misunderstood. Jeff shook his head. "No, *you* were. You're the one who's supposed to say it. 'I was wrong,'" he repeated, prompting her.

She lifted her chin stubbornly. "I wasn't wrong to leave Belle's Grove."

He detected the wavering in her voice. It wasn't so cut-and-dried for her anymore. It was all he wanted to hear. "But?"

Time was evaporating. She looked up the stairs, but knew Jeff would block her way until he heard her say it. "I was wrong to leave with Cal. Wrong not to let you know. Wrong to let you find out by word of mouth the way you did." She ran out of breath. "Okay?"

"Okay." His expression softened as he looked at her dress. The bodice clung to her every breath. "You look sexy in that dress."

She shrugged self-consciously, knowing she should go, wanting to linger a second longer. She was quickly running out of seconds. Permanently. "I'm supposed to look competent, not sexy."

"Why?"

She searched for a reason and discovered that she really didn't have any that made sense. "This is a wedding and I'm handling it."

She was wearing that cologne again, the one that made his senses swim. "Competent can be very sexy."

How could she argue with that? "You're hopeless, you know that?"

Her shoulders were bare. He ran his hand along them and watched her respond. "On the contrary, I am nothing if not hopeful." He let her back away this time. It was time to get Emmett. "See you at the head of the line, gorgeous."

She had one foot on the stairs. "That's for the bride and groom," Carole Anne corrected.

She might have saved her breath. He winked at her. "Yeah, I know."

Carole Anne gave up. "Just get everyone out into the backyard, will you?"

"Consider it done."

A very small voice bid Carole Anne to come in when she knocked. Connie was sitting on her bed in her wedding gown, her hands knotted together. No bride, Carole Anne thought with pride, ever looked lovelier.

Connie looked up at her niece and gave her a quirky little half smile. "I think I'm finally getting those prewedding jitters you were talking about."

Carole Anne's heart went out to Aunt Connie. She thought of the houseful of guests and a touch of panic tempered the sympathy.

What would she tell them if—?

"Second thoughts?" Carole Anne asked, concerned for more reasons than one.

Connie looked at her, puzzled. Why would she have second thoughts about marrying someone as wonderful as Emmett? She picked at a snag in her comforter. "Oh, no, never that. I'm just afraid of tripping while walking down the aisle."

Carole Anne squelched the desire to laugh in relief. She patted her aunt's hand. "Take small steps, you'll be fine."

Connie laughed softly. "Hard thing to do when you're eager."

"You'll manage." Carole Anne flew to the doorway. It was time to tell the organist to begin. Crossing the threshold, she hesitated, then turned around and reentered the room again.

Connie looked up at her in surprise as Carole Anne sat down next to her on the bed. She embraced her aunt. "I love you, Aunt Connie."

Touched, Connie sniffled and hugged her niece in response. "I love you, too."

Carole Anne released her. There was a wedding to get under way. No time for sentiment or overwhelming emotions of any type. Just the truth. "I'm so glad you found someone to love."

Connie beamed, smoothing her dress with loving strokes. "It was a nice surprise, wasn't it?" She looked at her niece meaningfully. "Life can be full of nice surprises, you know, if you let it."

Carole Anne rolled her eyes, but she was smiling. "Not another plug for Jeff."

"You'll find your own way, dear. You don't need any more prodding from me." Connie rose from the bed, glancing at her reflection in the wardrobe mirror. She picked up her bouquet of white daisies and pink carnations. "Well, I'm ready."

Yes, Carole Anne thought as she pushed herself from the bed, she was. Giving the silken cheek a quick kiss, Carole Anne moved to the doorway. "I'll go and tell them to start."

Carole Anne caught Jeff's eye as she walked into the backyard. He raised a questioning brow and she responded by giving him a slight nod. They were ready to begin.

Turning, she looked toward the organist seated near the house. "Okay, you can begin."

The first strains of the wedding march floated through the still air when suddenly the sky was filled with wings. Dove wings. Richard had released the doves and they were everywhere.

"Oh, God." Carole Anne groaned.

Brandon had started down the long, white runner that led from the house to the floral-encrusted arch where the minister stood waiting. Quickly, Carole Anne signaled for him to stop. Brandon, balancing the two rings on a satin pink pillow, looked at his mother curiously, then laughed in sheer delight as he watched the doves cover the sky. Folding chairs were being shifted right and left to get a better view.

Carole Anne hurried to the side of the house. Richard had just opened the last of his cages. "What are you doing?" she cried.

He rose to his feet, confused. "You said to begin."

"That was for the organist, not you." She could have shot him. "The doves were supposed to be released at the *end* of the ceremony."

Richard muttered something about it not being *his* fault as he slammed the cage shut.

A gentling hand was on her shoulder. She turned to find Jeff behind her. "It's different." He nodded at Richard, then took Carole Anne aside, almost forcibly dragging her away. "We'll wing it from here."

She shot him a murderous look. "That had to be the world's worst pun."

"Best I can come up with now."

Carole Anne sighed as she looked at the sky. The doves had begun returning to their cages. "I supposed it could be worse. Ham and his friends could have used the doves for target practice when they were released."

"There you go." Jeff nodded. "Always a silver lining."

Yes, there she went, she thought, straight into the insane asylum. She scanned the sky. The last of the doves was flying back to its cage. The guests were shifting their chairs back into position, facing front, waiting for act two to begin.

Carole Anne blew out a breath. Only Aunt Connie's wedding, she thought, shaking her head. She saw Mrs. Matthews, the organist, looking at her quizzically as she mimicked Carole Anne's movement.

"No," Carole Anne mouthed. "Go ahead." She gestured with her hands. "Play."

To her relief, the strains of the wedding march began again. The chatter settled down.

This was going to be the last wedding she was *ever* going to be involved in, Carole Anne swore to herself, taking her position on the minister's right.

A hush fell over everyone.

She didn't think she'd cry.

Shows what she knew, she thought ruefully. The tears had started smarting her eyes the moment she saw Brandon marching slowly down the aisle. They materialized in earnest by the time her aunt emerged, looking timelessly beautiful.

"Careful, people are going to think that you're sentimental," Jeff whispered in her ear.

She sniffled and wished for a handkerchief. "I think I'm just allergic to pigeons."

Jeff fished out his handkerchief and passed it to her as the minister pronounced Aunt Connie and Emmett husband and wife. "They were doves."

She wiped her eyes and handed the handkerchief back to him. "Whatever."

Bulbs went off as a professional photographer Aunt Connie had once baby-sat commemorated the moment for her keepsake album. Applause followed from the guests as Emmett kissed the bride. More flashes.

Jeff leaned toward Carole Anne. "We won't have doves at our wedding," he promised.

All around them chairs were being folded and pulled aside per Carole Anne's previous instructions to Ham and his crew. But it was happening without her watchful supervision. Carole Anne was too busy blocking Jeff with countermoves.

"We're not having a wedding," she snapped. "We're not having a relationship." The band she had hired was starting

AUNT CONNIE'S WEDDING 161

to play. She heard only her own heart pounding. "We're not having anything, do you hear me?"

"Whatever you say," he answered amiably.

As if it would be that easy. She wanted to punch him again.

The desire to swing at his chiseled jaw left as Jeff took her into his arms. Then only the nervous skittishness remained. "What are you doing?" she demanded under her breath.

"We're the best man and matron of honor. This is the first dance. We're supposed to join in, remember?" Jeff nodded toward Aunt Connie and Emmett.

She'd been so busy attempting to hold Jeff at bay she hadn't realized that they were not in the center of the area reserved for dancing. Or that the "Anniversary Song" was being played. Next to them, the newest married couple in Belle's Grove was dancing and silently pledging their undying love with their eyes for all their friends and neighbors to see.

Embarrassed, Carole Anne flushed. "Of course, I remember."

She slid her hand into his, then shifted and looked up at him in surprise. He only grinned in response to the look in her eyes. Carole Anne felt herself growing warmer.

"You're holding me too close, Jeff," she protested. Carole Anne looked around, afraid that others were noticing, as well.

If they did, they didn't make any indication. Emmett and Connie appeared to have everyone's attention.

"Not nearly close enough, Carole Anne," Jeff whispered against her ear, sending shock waves through her system. "Not nearly close enough."

She attempted to wedge a distance between them, and couldn't. "Any closer and I'd be in your breast pocket."

There was amusement in his eyes. "Would that be so bad?"

His words feathered along her face, dissolving any shred of resistance she was attempting to gather to her. "Maybe not, but not here."

Slowly, he slid his hands along her back. Her shiver pleased him. He was getting to her. Little by little, he was getting to her.

"I could meet you later."

She shook her head. "I have to clean up."

"Later," he repeated.

She felt herself wavering, but held fast. No more mistakes. "After that, I have to pack."

He looked into her eyes, searching for something he'd only recognize when he found it. "Still leaving?"

She slowly nodded her head. Her throat felt dry. "I have to."

"Why?"

The same question had begun to echo in her head. She tried vainly to remember her answer. "Because my job is there, and my life."

"Your life," he told her, suddenly whirling her around the floor to the applause of the guests who were watching, "is anywhere you are."

Why are you putting me through this? "I don't have time for Philosophy 101, Jeff. I have to get back. There's a story deadline."

He laced his fingers through hers, as if that would keep her here. "You can plug in anywhere. Last time I looked, Belle's Grove had just gotten electricity."

She dug in, but felt as if there was only quicksand beneath her feet. "I don't know about electricity, but Belle's Grove has got an obnoxious doctor who just won't give up."

"That's right," he agreed quietly. Jeff sounded all the more determined because of that. "I won't. Not again."

She wasn't going to win. That left only retreat. The music had stopped.

"If you'll excuse me—" she stepped back "—I think the dance is over." Carole Anne turned around and began to walk away. Quickly.

"Maybe, but the melody lingers on," Jeff called after her.

Now what the hell was that supposed to mean? she wondered.

Chapter Eleven

It was over.

All that madness, all that rushing around. The feverish scramble for sufficient tables and chairs for the reception. The wrong flowers being delivered and hurriedly exchanged. The doves released far too early. All of it was over.

Relief, not sadness, should be pervading her. Yet it wasn't. Carole Anne felt a bitter pang she couldn't explain lingering within her like a melody that refused to fade away as she hugged her aunt and new uncle.

She blinked back unexpected tears as she looked at her aunt in the pale blue two-piece suit she had purchased for her. Clearing her throat, she stepped back and looked at the newly pronounced Mr. and Mrs. Carson. "You two have a wonderful, wonderful time, you hear?"

"Tahiti." Aunt Connie sighed the name aloud with all the mystery and allure that befitted the tiny island. "I've never even been east of the Missouri border."

AUNT CONNIE'S WEDDING

Jeff grinned as he leaned over to her ear and prompted in a stage whisper, "Tahiti is west of us. It's in the Pacific Ocean."

The correction didn't faze her in the slightest. Aunt Connie never minded being wrong, Carole Anne thought fondly. The woman would probably live forever.

"See?" Connie turned toward her new husband. "I don't know where anything is."

Emmett sandwiched her small hand in his and patted it. "Well, I'm going to enjoy showing you everything," he promised.

Aunt Connie giggled like a young bride in response.

Jeff glanced at his watch. "You two newlyweds had better save those long, lingering looks for the back of the car. Otherwise, you're going to miss the flight," he cautioned. As it was, he was going to have to ignore speed limits to get there.

Wedding guests were crowding in around Connie and Emmett, wishing them a safe trip and a good time. But Connie was aware of only her niece, seeing her through the eyes of a concerned parent.

"I hate to leave you with all this work, dear." Connie looked around the living room regretfully. Carole Anne was a stickler for neatness and Connie knew the girl wouldn't rest until everything was in order again. She glanced at Jeff. There were far more important things in life than a clean house.

Carole Anne had already received more than half a dozen offers to help with cleanup. "Don't worry, I'll have plenty of help." She indicated the people in the room. "Everyone's pitching in. Now go. Go." She gestured toward the front door.

But Connie remained where she stood. A sadness had entered her eyes as she looked at her niece. "You won't be here when I get back, will you?" Connie asked softly.

Carole Anne slowly shook her head. "No, Brandon and I have to be going home. The wedding's over." Why in heaven's name did she feel like crying? What was the matter with her?

Connie nodded as she pressed her lips together. People around them slipped back, instinctively leaving the five people a moment of privacy. "Then this really is goodbye."

Carole Anne suddenly hated the sound of the word. Goodbye. It had to be the cruelest word in the English language.

"Emmett will bring you to L.A. to see us." She looked at Emmett for confirmation. The white leonine head nodded. "I insist," she told her aunt as she squeezed the older woman's hand. "Okay?"

Connie remained uncharacteristically silent. She was choking back tears as she turned to Brandon and opened her arms. The boy fell into them easily, comfortably, as if this was home for him.

Still fighting tears, Connie hugged Brandon to her ample bosom. "Take care of your mama," she instructed, releasing him. She struggled back to her feet.

Brandon smiled sheepishly, then stepped back, glancing toward Jeff. "I'm trying to do that."

Only Connie and Emmett saw his wink.

Connie sighed. "Goodbye, dear." She hugged Carole Anne again, wishing moments could last longer and that time could be something to paste into an album whose pages wouldn't yellow. "Be good to yourself." She patted Carole Anne's cheek. "And don't be afraid to rethink your decisions."

"The plane," Jeff prompted kindly.

"Come, Constance. They won't hold it for us, no matter how beautiful you look in that outfit." Gently, Emmett took his wife's elbow and ushered her out the door. Carole Anne followed them out, with Brandon hurrying next to her, waving madly.

She heard her aunt sniffling as she and Emmett walked to the car Jeff had rented for the occasion.

Jeff took Carole Anne's arm, drawing her attention to him. "I'll stop by when I get back from driving them to the airport." He searched her face, wanting to find a spark there that told him she *wanted* him to come by.

Carole Anne could only nod stiffly, fighting with emotions that were swallowing each other up and completely disorienting her. "Only if it's not too inconvenient for you," she murmured. She was trying very hard not to cry in front of him.

"Maybe it'll be too late to stop by," Jeff added, following Emmett and Connie down the stairs.

She had no idea what to make of his response, except, perhaps, that he was giving up on her.

The bitter pang within her expanded, eating bits and pieces of her away, making way for the hollowness that formed.

This was a happy time, she insisted to herself. Her aunt was going on her honeymoon with a perfectly wonderful man who adored her, and she would finally be able to get back to her own life. *Why* did she feel as if she had just lost her best friend? Worse, the very purpose for living?

At twenty-eight, she was too young for a mid-life crisis.

She watched her aunt wave from the back seat of the car until the car disappeared down the road. Carole Anne sighed. Time to get on with it.

"C'mon, Brandon, there's lots of work to be done." She took his hand and began to usher him into the house.

Brandon had had other plans for the rest of the day. "Aw, Mom."

"Work builds character, Brandon." She purposely hid her smile as she crossed the threshold, Brandon's hand firmly in hers.

"I guess there're a lot of characters here, then, huh, Mom?" He looked at all the women in the living room, wedding guests who had reverted back to the role of friends. They were all busy helping Carole Anne clean up.

She was speechless at the sight until she remembered that this was the way things were done here. It seemed that everyone who had helped to set up and decorate the house and grounds was now working to take it all down. It reminded Carole Anne of a wedding she had attended when just into her teens.

Nostalgia flooded through her like honey, clear and golden. She had to stop doing this to herself, she thought, but to no avail.

Carole Anne gave assignments to Brandon and his friends. Everyone else worked without being told what to do, like a well-oiled machine. They made good progress.

She was surprised to see the florist's van pull up in the driveway. Why was the man returning? She'd paid the bill right at the outset.

The tall, thin man scratched the tiny bald patch at the top of his head and flushed as he cleaned his feet on the mat at the front door. As she watched him, it reminded her of a mating ritual for some tall, exotic, rare bird. The man pushed the screen open and nodded toward the baskets of flowers by the staircase before he looked at Carole Anne.

"With the mix-up and everything, I, um, forgot to tell you that I'll be here later—I mean, now. I mean—" He cleared his throat and started again. "I came to pick up any of the baskets you don't want."

It seemed to her like an odd thing to do. "You reuse them?"

"No, ma'am." His Adam's apple bobbed like a pinball that had been knocked into play. "We take them over to the next town. The convalescent hospital uses them to brighten up the patients' rooms."

Generosity of spirit. How many times had she thought of that as hopelessly cornball and boring? She felt ashamed. Carole Anne urged the man over to the flower arrangements.

"Sure. I won't have any need of them and Aunt Connie's going to be gone for—"

Carole Anne stopped. Habit ingrained from long standing cautioned her to refrain from mentioning that the house was going to be empty for a space of time.

Then she flushed. That sort of thinking applied to L.A., not Belle's Grove. Here the doors weren't even locked at night unless it was to keep a fierce winter wind from blowing through.

"Two weeks," she concluded. "So you're welcome to them all. When you finish here, you can have the ones in the backyard, as well." She paused. "Do you need any help?"

"No, I'm fine, thanks." The man waved her away as he got started.

Looking around the living room, she felt a little like a fifth wheel. Well, there were other things to see to. She hurried out to the kitchen, needing to be of some use. If she was busy, she couldn't think.

In the kitchen, the three women who had catered the affair were busy packing up the leftovers for Carole Anne. The stack on the kitchen table began to resemble skyscrapers in the making. Carole Anne thought about having each guest take some food home with them.

"Something wrong?" As she asked, Rita Renfield expertly mummified a tray of crackers and cheese in crystal pink cellophane. A doer, it had initially been Rita's idea to start the catering business.

Carole Anne shook her head. "No, everything was wonderful. It's just that I don't have any use for all this food." She glanced at the refrigerator. It wasn't even large enough to accommodate the leftovers. "Not to mention, not enough space. It seems a shame to let it all go to waste."

Rita exchanged looks with the other two women.

"Well," Rita began slowly, "if you don't want to keep it, we wouldn't mind taking it down to the trailer park for you." The momentum in her voice, not to mention her enthusiasm, picked up. "A few of the families there aren't doing too well. They could certainly use this." She indicated the table.

Carole Anne had forgotten how the people of Belle's Grove always prided themselves on taking care of their own. What else had she forgotten, she thought, living out in Los Angeles?

"By all means." She opened the cupboard and took out another roll of cellophane wrap.

Rita took it from her like a benevolent teacher confiscating a stick from a child in the school yard. "No, that's all right, don't trouble yourself. We've got everything under control. The girls and I are used to doing this. We can manage everything here. I'm sure you have a lot of other things to do."

Rita all but threw her out of her own kitchen. Or rather, Carole Anne thought, leaving, what used to be her kitchen. She was only visiting now and had no right to claim anything here.

But she wanted to, she realized, the pang taking shape slowly. It was almost identifiable now. Almost, but not quite.

Rita was wrong. Carole Anne didn't have a lot of other things to see to. She discovered that as soon as she walked into the backyard.

Ham and his crew were far more apt at taking down the huge tent they had used at the reception than they had been at setting it up. The job went twice as fast, she noted. And the tables and chairs she had borrowed were all returning home with their owners.

The backyard had been picked clean of the occasional scrap of litter by Brandon and his friends.

AUNT CONNIE'S WEDDING

There was nothing for her to do, no way to lose herself in work.

Restless, Carole Anne tried the living room again.

It was a hive of activity. The festive decorations were being unwound from the staircase, taken down from the walls, unstrung from the doorways. Carole Anne stood still for a moment, in awe of all this efficiency. She felt a wave of guilt over the thoughts she had once had about these people, believing them inept, hopelessly backward and unsophisticated. Here they were, helping her out, brightening up strangers' lives with leftover flowers, feeding their own when need be. Making life a little better for everyone. There wasn't anything unsophisticated about that.

She was the unsophisticated one for believing that geography equaled worldliness.

Janice turned around, a freshly rewound roll of crepe paper in her hand. She saw the oddly pensive look on Carole Anne's face, and walked up to her.

"What's up?"

Embarrassed, Carole Anne quickly covered for herself. "You really don't have to do all this, you know," she said to Janice.

"Why?" Janice laughed away Carole Anne's protest. She dropped the crepe paper into the box that had originally contained the decorations. "It gives me a chance to catch up on gossip and, most important, to get away from the kids. Brett took the little darlings home half an hour ago." She sighed as if she was in a state of euphoria. "I may just stay here overnight."

Her proclamation was met with a chorus of agreement from the other women in the room.

A grown-up slumber party, Carole Anne thought giddily. She looked at the women, working the idea out. Even with the caterers taking the food, there was still plenty left in the refrigerator to satisfy a midnight run. Aunt Connie had forgotten to clean it out.

"You could, you know," Carole Anne told them. A few of the women stopped to listen. "I'm not leaving until morning. You could all stay over."

It sounded tempting, but Janice spoke for all of them when she turned the invitation down.

"Don't tempt a desperate woman, Carole Anne. The only thing more desperate than me right now wishing for a little space is me tomorrow morning, looking at the state of chaos in my kitchen. Brett's a wonderful provider." She lowered her voice. "And a great lover."

A few muffled, good-natured comments buzzed behind her, but Janice purposely ignored them. "But he can't cook worth a darn, and as for cleaning—" she rolled her eyes dramatically "—the twister in *The Wizard of Oz* did a better job of straightening up than he does.

"No." Janice sighed regretfully. "I'd better get back to my man." She squeezed Carole Anne's arm affectionately, remembering when they had shared harmless secrets and dreams at all-night slumber parties. "But thanks for the offer."

Janice stood back and surveyed the area. The living room was restored to order. She nodded, satisfied. "I guess that does it, ladies." She turned to Carole Anne. "Anything else you want done before we leave?"

Carole Anne laughed and shook her head. "I could use you in my condo in L.A."

"Sorry, the commute would kill me." Janice kissed her friend's cheek. With luck, Brett had put the kids to bed and she could actually enjoy an evening with him. But she doubted it. "Well, don't be such a stranger," she chided fondly. "Don't make it so long between visits next time."

To a symphony of goodbyes, the other women left ahead of Janice.

"It was great seeing you again. Oh—" Janice turned to look at Carole Anne "—any chance of seeing our names in print after all this?"

Carole Anne grinned, thinking primarily of the doves. Now that the incident and the wedding were all behind her, the whole affair took on the tone that humor pieces were made of.

She nodded, pieces of the article already taking shape in her mind. "A very distinct possibility."

Janice squealed with delight. Carole Anne's success in getting her articles published in major magazines had always been a source of vicarious pride with her.

"Wait until I tell Brett. He always figured that you'd get gobbled up out there in L.A." She let triumph color her expression. "Said the place attracted hopefuls like a magnet and then had them for breakfast."

From where she stood right now, it sounded like an apt description to Carole Anne. No, that wasn't fair. After all, she had made it. She had her own byline in a semi-monthly magazine, she did free-lance work for major publications, she had three coffee table books out, and there was this screenplay idea she was kicking around.

A screenplay.

Maybe...

"I am so *proud* of you. Well, I've got to hustle. See you." Janice hurried out of the house just as Rita came up behind Carole Anne.

"I left you some of the wedding cake," the older woman told Carole Anne. "It always tastes so good for breakfast." She laughed, patting her own rather full figure. "As you can see. And there's a tray of hors d'oeuvres on the table in case you want to nibble later tonight." She began to retreat into the kitchen to take the leftovers out to their truck in the back. "The people at the trailer park are certainly going to be grateful to you."

She didn't have anything to do with it, Carole Anne thought. "You're the one who suggested it," she pointed out.

Rita stopped, one hand on the swinging door. "I could suggest until I'm blue in the face. *You* made the decision." Rita studied her for a moment. Carole Anne had gone to school with her Ruth and the two had played in each other's houses for years. Rita knew her as well as anyone. "Don't downplay yourself, Carole Anne." The woman's smile was motherly. "That was always your trouble, you know. You saw things black and white. Gray and beige work well, too. And my favorite, of course, is blue-gray." She patted Carole Anne's hand. "Before I go, I want you to know that I think you turned out very nicely."

The compliment sounded good, Carole Anne thought, pleasure spilling through her.

One by one, Aunt Connie's wedding guests left, restoring order in their wake. Restoring it everywhere but within her soul.

There, Carole Anne thought, shutting the door behind the last guest, it felt like a total disaster area. Hollow. Desolate.

Empty-nest blues. She laughed softly to herself. Wait until Brandon got married. Then she'd *really* feel it. But at least that was far and away in the future.

She looked up when she heard the noise. Brandon was coming down the stairs, a rolled-up blanket under one arm, a sack packed with "essentials" dragging behind him. It bumped down each step as he went.

"Hey—" she crossed to him "—where are you going?"

He looked at his mother impatiently. The itchy suit was a thing of the past and he was now wearing a striped T-shirt and shorts. "The sleep-over," he answered. "At Jimmy's house. Remember?"

That's right, she'd given him permission to spend the night next door. When she had agreed, she had been on the phone to the seamstress, checking on the last-minute alterations, and completely distracted. More important, she hadn't realized just how empty the house was going to feel after everyone left.

"Yes, but I thought..." Her voice trailed off as she tried to think of an excuse to make him want to stay. "I thought that maybe you and I could watch a movie and—"

She saw his face fall a little. Resigned, Brandon took a step back toward the stairs, ready to put his blanket and sack away.

What was she doing, forcing her son to stay at home because she was having trouble dealing with things emotionally? Carole Anne did a quick about-face and regrouped.

She snapped her fingers. "Hey, never mind. I just suddenly remembered I've got some things to catch up on. Writing stuff," she quickly added, knowing Brandon wouldn't question it beyond that. After all, writing was how she made her living and he understood there were times it had to come first. "I'm afraid I won't be able to watch the movie with you, after all."

He was already halfway out the door. "Great. I mean, um, you sure?"

She smiled. He'd make a lousy poker player. "I'm sure."

His eyes were bright. "'Cause Jimmy's my bestest friend forever and ever—after Dr. Jeff—and you."

Maybe not a poker player, but a born diplomat, she thought fondly. "You know, this is the first time you ever slept over at anyone's house," she realized aloud. Brandon had had invitations before, but he had always turned them down. She suspected it was because he was afraid to be separated from her overnight for some reason.

The slender shoulders rose and fell in a pronounced shrug. "I figure I'm old enough."

"Yes," she said on a sigh, "you are." She opened the screen door as he struggled with his things. "Have a good time."

"Bye, Mom." Brandon trudged out, secure and content in his newfound independence. Then he stopped, dropped the blanket and sack to the ground and hurried back to her. "Sorry." He quickly kissed her cheek and gave her a hug. "Almost forgot."

"As long as you didn't," she said, her heart brimming with love for the little man she had managed to raise on her own. *Not bad even if I do say so myself.*

She closed the door slowly.

The house felt bigger, emptier. Lonelier than it ever had before.

She felt very sorry for herself, although she hadn't a clue as to why. Her aunt was married, and her son was finally behaving like a normal little boy. And tomorrow, they'd be on the plane to Los Angeles, getting back to her work and to everything she loved.

Cared for.

Everything she was used to, she amended, downgrading the assessment one more time.

Carole Anne moved about the house slowly, like a spring breeze passing through. There was nothing to do. Everyone had done it for her. Look as she might, she couldn't find anything amiss. There wasn't so much as a flower petal to pick up from the floor, a piece of crepe paper to unstick from the wall. A dish in the sink to wash.

Done. It was all done.

Except for the packing.

Carole Anne sighed. She might as well get to it.

She turned and headed for the stairs. But she couldn't make herself go past the third step. She didn't want to go upstairs and pack now. Maybe later.

A depression hung around her, covering her like a thick, coarse mantle. There was no sense of urgency to pack and leave, the way there had once been all those years ago. Even the way there had been the first day she arrived for Aunt Connie's wedding. She didn't feel the need to "escape" any longer.

Carole Anne skimmed a finger absently down the railing as she planted both feet on the floor. No, she didn't want to leave Belle's Grove this time, she realized. But she was a realist. Being here was just a holiday. She had a life to return to. She had left here in the first place because it was all too confining to her, too small-townish. She liked the hectic promise that throbbed within a big city. That throbbed within Los Angeles.

She wandered aimlessly through the kitchen, feeling an odd disquiet churning inside. She didn't know what to do with herself, where to go. She wished Janice had stayed. She needed someone to talk to.

Without meaning to, she went outside and sat down in the gazebo. Crickets were calling to each other. They might have been playing the *1812* Overture for all she heard. She was too busy sorting out her thoughts.

What did she *really* have in L.A. beyond the noise and the stress-inducing pace? Fleeting friendships and relationships that never went beyond the superficial. Of course, she had never allowed the relationships to flourish because of Cal.

She frowned. If there *had* been someone special, he would have penetrated that wall of hers no matter what obstacles she put up.

The way Jeff had.

No, it wouldn't do her any good to think about Jeff. She had no options available to her there. She and Jeff had a past that would rise up and haunt them if she allowed herself to get serious.

She meant what she had said to him earlier. She hadn't been wrong to leave Belle's Grove when she did. If she hadn't, she would have always gone on wondering what she was missing, gone on resenting life here instead of appreciating it for what it was.

A tiny little jewel sparkling in a world gone slightly haywire.

But she *had* been wrong to leave it with Cal. Cal with his dark, brooding eyes, his sensuous poet's mouth and his empty promises. Most of all, she'd been wrong to leave Jeff the way she had, without even a note. It was that sense of desperation that had overcome her, the fear of living and dying in a small town without ever having sampled anything else, anything more. And Cal had promised more, so very much more.

He'd promised her the moon hanging from a silver charm bracelet.

Jeff had promised her only stability. But what she had mistaken for feet of clay was really a wonderful sense of responsibility, of compassion tempered with a passion she was unaware of.

But it was too late for regrets and what-if's. Her path was forged, her life set. She had a wonderful son and had made something of herself. She couldn't expect to strike it rich in all three areas. She couldn't expect to be lucky in love, as well.

Jeff and Brandon got along now, but what if he wound up looking at the boy's face day after day, seeing Cal there? Seeing the imprint of the man who had caused her to run out on him? How could they survive something like that? What would it do to them as a family? *Would* they be a family?

It was too much to ask of any of them.

Besides, she thought, winding her arms around herself, feeling a chill that wasn't in the air, Jeff hadn't returned from the airport to see her. He had told her he would, and he hadn't.

She was acting like a whiny child, she upbraided herself. It was better like this. Better to break it clean now, without a scene. If she was lucky, she wouldn't see Jeff before she left tomorrow.

She rocked quietly as dusk slowly crept up and dimmed the world. She finally put a name to the bitter pang she was feeling. It was homesickness. And she hadn't even left yet.

Carole Anne didn't realize that her cheeks were wet or that she was crying.

Chapter Twelve

There was no use in putting off the inevitable. Packed or not, she still had to go back to L.A. tomorrow, so she might as well get to it. There were two tickets in her purse for the return flight, and a story waiting on a disk by her computer to complete. Aunt Connie was on her way to Tahiti and there was absolutely no reason for Carole Anne to stay any longer.

No logical reason.

With the desperation of a drowning man trying to seize anything that would help keep him afloat, she reminded herself that she had learned to appreciate logic and eschew most emotions. Emotions only got you into trouble. She smiled ruefully. Her emotions had ruled her head, causing her to ignore all of Cal's shortcomings until they finally overcame her.

Carole Anne sighed and rose. There was no use looking back, only forward.

She went inside the house and up to her room.

Her room.

It had a nice ring to it. The room evoked so many memories. The gesture to preserve the room the way it had been, instead of turning it into a sewing room or a den, meant a great deal to Carole Anne. It had felt good, she thought as she slowly, methodically, folded a pair of shorts until they were one-eighth their normal size, to come home.

She looked around the room as if seeing it for the first time since she had left. *This* was home, not her pristine condo in L.A. And this would always be home. Because this was where her heart really was. This is where she felt safe and warm and loved.

Jeff had been right.

Jeff had been right about a lot of things. Carole Anne sighed deeply.

She was just making herself crazy, Carole Anne thought. Frustrated, confused, she balled up a blouse and threw it into the open suitcase on her bed. And missed. It fell onto the floor.

"New way to pack?"

She swung around, startled. Jeff was in the doorway, leaning a shoulder against the doorjamb. How long had he been standing there, watching her? She felt like a fool. "What are you doing here?"

"Discovering that you're not in any danger of being first draft pick for any major basketball team." Crossing to her, Jeff picked up the blouse. Rather than place it in the suitcase, he elaborately hung it back up in the closet. "You left the front door open."

She yanked the blouse off the hanger and dropped it, unfolded, into the suitcase. She'd iron when she got to L.A. "No, I didn't."

"I haven't learned to pick locks, yet," he informed her quietly. "So that means you left the door open. Like you used to." He smiled. "You're slipping into your old habits again."

His voice was low, seductive, as he came up behind her. Brushing her hair slowly away from her neck, he leaned over and softly pressed a kiss there.

Carole Anne felt her bones dissolving as if they had been dipped in a chemical solution. "Don't," she breathed.

"Why?" With slow, achingly deliberate precision, he worked his way to the other side of her neck. Her skin tasted sweet, inviting, like berries in the fall. "I want to develop some new habits with you so we can make them into old habits soon." He felt her shiver against him and felt his own aroused response. "Very soon."

With more effort than she had ever mustered before, Carole Anne pulled away. "It's too late for that."

But he wasn't about to be put off, not with any excuses, least of all flimsy ones. "It's nine-thirty. The evening is young."

She swung around to look at him accusingly. "You know what I mean."

"No, I don't." His expression grew serious, almost dangerous. A town could have lit up from the charged electricity between them, she thought. "Why don't you tell me what you mean?"

She clenched her hands at her sides. All right, it was finally time to face this, to have it out. She'd be gone tomorrow, she knew she didn't have to look him in the eyes after tonight. "I know how deeply I hurt you by leaving. It's a wound that can't ever be mended."

His eyes were dark, stormy, as he looked at her. She almost took a step back, afraid. "Let's get something straight, okay? You have no *idea* how much you hurt me when you left. I felt as if someone had ripped up my insides with shards of broken glass. I felt betrayed, and more alone than I ever had in my whole life. I *died* inside."

This was even worse than she had thought. Carole Anne turned, fighting tears, wanting to get away. His hand clamped onto her wrist, holding her prisoner. Cupping her face, Jeff forced her to look at him.

The darkness had given way to something else. There was a warmth there now, bathing her, as if she was the one who needed to be soothed instead of him. "You also have no idea how well I can mend. Only I can know that."

She didn't bother wiping away her tears. "I'm sorry," she said hoarsely. If only she knew how to make it up to him. "I don't know what to say. I'm sorry, so very, very sorry."

"That part is over." There was a finality in his voice that closed a door. He released her arm and stepped back.

Regrets, remorse, all flooded through her. But it was too late. He had just said so. She had no right to ask for a second chance. "I know."

He saw that she misunderstood. "Not the feelings, Carole Anne, just the event."

She looked at him, surprised. Confused.

For a moment he refrained from touching her. She needed to hear this and he needed to say it. Touching her would make him forget everything but the longing that was there.

"I know now that you had to go. You probably wouldn't have become what you are today if you had stayed here, waiting for me to come home every night. What's worse, you would have resented me and what we had wouldn't have blossomed. It would have curdled like milk left out on the counter in the sun." He shrugged philosophically, still keeping distance between them.

"So now you've become what you had the potential to become, and seen what you wanted to see." He spread his hands wide for emphasis. "You've had travel and city life for eight years." He paused, his eyes searching her face. "Do you really want to go back to it?"

There was no point in lying or trying to keep up a facade. Not with Jeff. He saw things all too clearly. And she didn't want to pretend. Not with him. Not even with herself. "No."

He leaned against the bureau, his arms crossed in front of him. "Well, then?"

Frustration balled up fists within her. "It's not that simple."

He didn't see why things had to be complicated, why restrictions had to be applied. "Why? Why isn't it that simple?"

She threw up her hands, pacing like a caged animal at the zoo, seeing the way out but unable to take it. "Because things never are."

He laughed shortly. She couldn't tell if there was mirth in his laugh or not. "Now you're tap-dancing with logic. It won't work, not with me."

She licked her lips, tempted, oh, so tempted, to surrender. "What if it *doesn't* work?"

She'd become so negative since she had left Belle's Grove, he thought. He was going to have to work to restore her to her former frame of mind, lovingly, just as he had restored the clinic.

Jeff took her hand, then brought it to his lips and kissed it. "Then we'll deal with it. But it's not a mistake. I only made one mistake after that initial one of leaving you with Cal. I only have one regret. That I didn't go after you when I heard that you and Cal were divorced." He let out a sigh, baring his soul to her. "I let my pride get in my way. I wanted you to see how if felt to be abandoned." He looked into her eyes, looking for forgiveness for them both. "For that, I was wrong."

"No, you weren't." She touched his cheek. He deserved to feel that way, after what she had done to him. It was something she had believed, even then. And regretted.

He shook his head, contradicting her. "Wasted time." He said the words ruefully. "But that's behind us. I don't want to waste the future. I'm not going to let my pride make me make a second mistake and allow you to leave without speaking my mind."

He placed his hands on her shoulders, his eyes holding her mesmerized. "I love you, Carole Anne. I have always loved you and I always will until the day I die." A smile creased his lips. "Longer if I can find a way. And in your heart—" he lightly traced the pattern on her breast, making her heart skip "—you know you love me, too. All you have to do," he coaxed, "is admit it."

She wanted to. With all her heart, she wanted to. But there wasn't just herself to think of. "Brandon—"

He stopped her before she got any further. "Brandon is a great kid. I want to be a father to him." He saw the tears gather in her eyes again. "A boy deserves to have a father who loves him."

She must have misunderstood. She couldn't be this lucky. Once she would have thought so, but experience had been a hard, cruel teacher. "Loves him?" she echoed.

He nodded, not seeing what the difficulty was. "He's part of you, isn't he?"

She could hardly get the word out. "Yes."

He stood watching her as she began to move restlessly around again. He spoke without skipping a beat. "That would be enough for me, but he's pretty neat in his own right, as well."

It was all too good to be true. And she had learned that things that were too good to be true generally weren't. "And if I said no to this?"

Jeff straightened, hooking his thumbs in his jeans. "I'll drive you to the airport."

If he gave up so quickly, he didn't mean what he had just said. "I see."

He lifted her chin with the tip of his finger until her eyes were raised to his. "And then I'd hijack the plane."

She was silent for a moment, and she saw the affirmation in his eyes. And a great deal more. "You'd do it, too, wouldn't you?"

"I'd do anything I had to to keep you in my life." Comfortably, he drew her into his arms. This time, she didn't resist. The last test was over. And she had aced the exam. Because of him. "Beg, kidnap, whatever. I told you before, you're mine, Carole Anne, and I'm yours. Nothing you can do can ever change that. I don't care about the past. I only care about now. And you. I want you in my life, Carole Anne. From this day forward."

She was beginning to believe that. And take huge comfort in the fact. "So you think you know that I love you, huh?"

He grinned easily. "Yep!"

This time, mischief, not resistance, curved her mouth. "Not that you're right, of course, but how do you know?"

Jeff attempted to look perfectly serious. "You know when you bent over to make that first shot in the billiard parlor?"

She watched him, curious. "Yes?"

"You wiggled that rear end of yours just a little more than the shot warranted." He grinned. "I knew it was for my benefit."

She lifted her chin defensively. "Did not."

He grazed her chin with his tongue and heard her moan. "Did, too."

She sighed, suddenly content to remain like this forever. "I swore I'd never plan another wedding after today."

That was fine with him. "Then I'll plan it." He brushed his lips over hers. She snuggled into him. "And since I'm planning it—"

"Yes?"

He kissed her again to prevent any more arguments from sprouting on her lips. "I'd like to start with the honeymoon first. Just a sample, mind you." His eyes teased hers.

Lightly, reverently, he caressed her, making her warm, making her anticipate. She leaned into him. "Sounds good to me."

Before she let herself slip completely away into the heat generated by his mouth, she had to tell him, had to say what had been singing in her veins now for days, she realized. "I love you, Jeff."

"Yeah, I know." He smiled into her eyes. "I always knew you did. You were just a little slow on the uptake, but we can handle that."

She had no doubts that they could handle anything. Together.

* * * * *

**HE'S MORE THAN
A MAN, HE'S
ONE OF OUR**

Fabulous Fathers

**THE BIRDS AND THE BEES
by Liz Ireland**

Bachelor Kyle Weston was going crazy—why else would he be daydreaming about marriage and children? At first he thought it was beautiful Mary Moore—and the attraction that still lingered twelve years after their brief love affair. Then Mary's daughter dropped a bombshell that shocked Kyle's socks off. Could it be young Maggie Moore was *his* child? Suddenly fatherhood was more than just a fantasy....

Join in the love—and the laughter—
in Liz Ireland's *THE BIRDS AND THE BEES*,
available in February.

Fall in love with our **FABULOUS FATHERS!**

Silhouette
ROMANCE™

FF294

Relive the romance...
Harlequin and Silhouette are proud to present

by Request™

A program of collections of three complete novels by the most requested authors with the most requested themes.

Available in February:

LOVER COME BACK!

It was over so long ago—yet now they're calling, "Lover, come back!"

Three complete novels in one special collection:

EYE OF THE TIGER by Diana Palmer
THE SHADOW OF TIME by Lisa Jackson
WHATEVER IT TAKES by Patricia Gardner Evans

Available wherever Silhouette® books are sold.

SREQ294

SPRING fancy '94

They're sexy, single...
and about to get snagged!

Passion is in full bloom as love catches
the fancy of three brash bachelors. You won't
want to miss these stories by three of
Silhouette's hottest authors:

**CAIT LONDON
DIXIE BROWNING
PEPPER ADAMS**

Spring fever is in the air this March—
and there's no avoiding it!

Only from Silhouette®

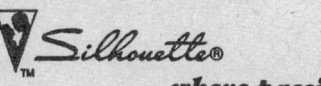

where passion lives.

SF94

**And now for
something completely different
from Silhouette....**

SPELLBOUND
R O M A N C E

Unique and innovative stories that take you into the world of paranormal happenings. Look for our special "Spellbound" flash—and get ready for a truly exciting reading experience!

**In February, look for
One Unbelievable Man (SR #993)
by Pat Montana.**

Was he man or myth? Cass Kohlmann's mysterious traveling companion, Michael O'Shea, had her all confused. He'd suddenly appeared, claiming she was his destiny—determined to win her heart. But could levelheaded Cass learn to believe in fairy tales...before her fantasy man disappeared forever?

Don't miss the charming, sexy and utterly mysterious
Michael O'Shea in
ONE UNBELIEVABLE MAN.
Watch for him in February—only from

Silhouette
R O M A N C E™

SPELL2

If you enjoyed this book by

MARIE FERRARELLA,

don't miss these other titles by this popular author!

Silhouette Romance™

#08920	BABIES ON HIS MIND	$2.69 ☐
#08932	THE RIGHT MAN	$2.69 ☐
#08947	IN HER OWN BACKYARD	$2.75 ☐
#08959	HER MAN FRIDAY	$2.75 ☐

Silhouette Special Edition®

#09703	SOMEONE TO TALK TO	$3.29 ☐
#09767	WORLD'S GREATEST DAD	$3.39 ☐
#09832	FAMILY MATTERS	$3.50 ☐
#09843	SHE GOT HER MAN	$3.50 ☐

Silhouette Intimate Moments®

#07496	HOLDING OUT FOR A HERO	$3.39 ☐
#07501	HEROES GREAT AND SMALL	$3.50 ☐

TOTAL AMOUNT	$
POSTAGE & HANDLING	$
($1.00 for one book, 50¢ for each additional)	
APPLICABLE TAXES*	$ _____
TOTAL PAYABLE	$ _____
(check or money order—please do not send cash)	

To order, complete this form and send it, along with a check or money order for the total above, payable to Silhouette Books, to: *In the U.S.:* 3010 Walden Avenue, P.O. Box 9077, Buffalo, NY 14269-9077; *In Canada:* P.O. Box 636, Fort Erie, Ontario, L2A 5X3.

Name: _____

Address: _____ City: _____

State/Prov.: _____ Zip/Postal Code: _____

*New York residents remit applicable sales taxes.
Canadian residents remit applicable GST and provincial taxes.

MFBACK5

Silhouette®